All We Ever Wanted

a love story

Seth King

Their relationship is forbidden.
Their union would be shocking.
But their love? It's undeniable…

Tommy Houston and James May are both nineteen when they are hired to sail a boat from Florida to Maine together.

Neither has ever been with another man before, and both come from highly traditional backgrounds. But as they sail up the coast, a sudden and overwhelming attraction explodes between them…

And over the next ten days on the open Atlantic, Tommy and James fall into a love so powerful, it comes to define both of their lives forever.

But how can they protect that love when their world wants nothing more than to pull them apart?

"Out beyond the ideas of right and wrong, there is a field. I'll meet you there."

-Rumi

for John

~

and for J + L

~

and lastly, for my great uncle and his "roommate"

2021

"So, by the way, I also just wanted to tell you that I'm gay."

My grandson Scott springs this on me on a totally normal phone call, only seconds after we were discussing his recent Spring Break trip with friends to Daytona. It stuns me and makes me drop the coffee mug I was holding, which shatters on the tile floor under me.

"Hello? Pappy?" Scott asks as the clatter rings out. "What in the world was *that*?"

"Oh, uh – sorry, I need a minute."

I totter over for the broom and then sweep up the ceramic shards, which of course isn't exactly easy at eighty-five years of age. I don't even bother mopping up the coffee, though – I want to know more.

"Sorry," Scott says when I come back to the phone. "I guess you threw something and broke some glass. I knew there was a chance you'd be mad...I'm sorry."

"*Mad*?" I ask, then I make up a white lie. "Oh, um – I'm not mad at all, my damned cat just sauntered in and knocked over a glass with her tail, that's all."

"Wait, really?" Scott asks me. "You're not mad? I just figured that because of...uh, your *age* and all...I know your generation has, uh, *different* views...since you came from a different time..."

"I'm an old fart," I smile. "You can say it. But of course I'm not *mad*. Tell me more, sonny."

"You really want to know more?"

I close my eyes. "I would *love* to know more."

"Okay, then..."

I listen as Scott tells me his story. Apparently he's been openly gay to his friends for years, but didn't want to rock the boat by telling this news to the older members of his family. But since he's going steady with a nice young man and about to move to "the gay part of town," as he calls it, he wanted to get it all out there to prevent anyone from coming across a photo of him on social media and getting a shock.

"And I really love Jay," he continues, "and I just wanted you to know I'm happy, and I'm sorry I didn't tell you sooner, and – wait, Pappy, are you *crying*?"

1

I pause and then realize that tears are streaming down my face. "Oh," I lie again. "Just, uh, just allergies, yes, I'm fine."

"Are you sure? It sounds like you're, well – *sobbing*."

I wipe my face. "No, sonny, I promise. I am very happy for you."

"Aw, thanks, Pappy!"

I lean forward. "Wait. Can…can I ask you a few questions?"

"Um. Of course, I guess?"

I clear my throat. "So, about all this gay business. You can just…you can…just run around town, being gay now?"

"Uh, yes," he sort of laughs. "Trust me, it's fine."

"Really? Nobody messes with you?"

"Hmm. I mean, once, some guy yelled out of his car that I was a faggot one night, but that was extremely true, and he was just some drunk frat boy, so I just posed and said thanks."

I laugh a little. "Very funny. How did your mother and father take it?"

"I dunno," he says casually. "They don't really care. They already knew. It's not like I was hiding it. It was kind of just unsaid knowledge."

I gasp.

"What?" Scott asks. "What is it?"

"Nothing, nothing. I'm just intrigued. So you…you and this boyfriend of yours…everyone in your social circle knows about it?"

"Well yeah, Pappy," he laughs. "That's kind of how it is these days. I just didn't know how the older generations of the family would react. I'm sorry."

I close my eyes again. "Well I love you, and I'm proud of you, and nothing would ever change that. Nothing in this world."

He inhales. "Thanks, Pappy. That really means a lot."

"Of course, my little Scottie."

After we say goodbye, I hang up the phone and cry for hours. I cry until my shirt is soaking wet, I cry until my cat is concerned, I cry until my youngest daughter, Carole, who comes to cook dinner for me twice a week, parks her car in the drive.

Damn, I think to myself. *How in the world would I explain* this *one…*

2

I finally get myself together enough to hide in the bathroom so Carole won't see me, and then I cry some more.

Listen to me when I say this, though:

I am not crying because I have a gay grandson.

I am not crying because I disapprove of him, or fear for him.

I am crying because in a way, I am *jealous* of him.

And that jealousy stems from the biggest secret of my life.

Oh, to have been born in a time when you could just call up a family member and mention, "by the way, I'm gay," like it's nothing, like you're discussing the weather…it fills me with an amount of regret and sadness I simply cannot put into words. It is unfathomable.

Because if *I* would've been lucky enough to have been born into a world like this, a world like Scott's, a world without shame…well, it would have changed my whole life.

Hell, it would've *given* me a life, period…

As Carole starts cooking something vaguely garlic-y in the kitchen, I sneak into my bedroom and unlock the safe in the back of my closet. I take out one of its only contents, a frayed, black-and-white photo of the man who defined my entire existence.

"Tommy," I cry as I hold the photo and run my wrinkled hands over his face. "Oh, Tommy…if only you could've heard that phone call…if only you knew…"

And then, my mind takes me back…

Part I
Before Him

"Love takes off the masks that we fear we cannot live without and know we cannot live within."

-James Baldwin

1956

"Why are you always looking at me like that, anyway?"

I looked away after the boy with the moonlight eyes asked me the question.

Why was I looking?

I was *looking* because he was the most beautiful thing I had ever seen.

It was April of 1956. I was in those aimless years after high school when I didn't quite know what I wanted to do with my life, or who I wanted to become. But I *did* know I liked the ocean, so at the time, I was working as a do-it-all deckhand at Mayport, my city's port and marina.

I was taking whatever jobs I could get, and a wealthy businessman wanted two young men to sail his sailboat from our city, Jacksonville, Florida, up the East Coast to his summer house in Maine. I was partnered with Tommy, whom I guessed was another poor young deckhand from town, looking for work. Up until now I'd avoided him as we'd readied the boat for departure, but finally he'd confronted me.

"Sorry," I finally said. "I tend to drift off into space sometimes."

He laughed, and it made his face even more stunning. His laugh sounded like music, it really did. "Don't mention it, space boy. I'm Tommy, by the way."

"James," I said, shaking his hand.

I knew he was trouble from that moment onward.

~

I cannot remember a time when I was not different. There wasn't really a vocabulary for it back then, but I did know that I was different. It wasn't until grammar school that I learned exactly *what* that difference was, and what it would mean for me and my life.

In the schoolyard one day, I heard one boy call another boy a queer.

"What's that? I asked him.

"What are you, slow or something?" he asked me. "It means when boys like boys, not girls. My dad said anyone like that should be killed."

5

I remember I shrank, physically shrank, after he said that – my shoulders sagged and my posture sank. For some reason I just felt an immediate need to take up a little less space in the world. I was like that boy, that "queer," and I knew it.

For some time, I was able to act like the other boys – I was able to hide, or at least avoid being noticed. But of course, what is natural cannot be contained.

When I was about ten, my father found me fooling around with another boy from down the street. We were just heavy-petting, experimenting, as kids sometimes do – but when my father slammed open my bedroom door asking if I'd seen the dog lately, I stopped breathing. My neighbor came to his senses and jumped out of the window as my dad took off his belt and started slowly walking toward my bed.

The welts on my body did not fade for weeks.

~

A few months later my father picked me up from school early. He told me we were going to see a very kind man who could help me. I was young enough to believe him.

We drove two hours to a very large university. After navigating a maze of corridors, we arrived at a very small office.

I sat at a table in one room with the man, while my dad sat in the neighboring room. A large window separated the two rooms. The man strapped me to a chair and then started attaching a series of wires to my wrists and ankles. I asked him what he was doing; he smiled and said he was helping me.

Once the wires were firmly attached, he turned on some kind of instrument. It reminded me of the earthquake monitors I'd seen in movies about California.

Then he took out a folder. He looked through the window at my father, who nodded. Then the man cleared his throat and pulled out a photo of a shirtless, muscular man. The instrument buzzed, and a sensation I'll never forget shot throughout my body – it was like the shock you get from touching a doorknob on a cold day, but a hundred times worse.

I writhed and squirmed; I urinated in my shorts and begged him to stop. He didn't.

It must've lasted an hour. The man kept taking out different photos of different men. Every time, the instrument would buzz.

And every time, the electricity would torture me anew.

On the way home, I could barely feel my body, and I passed out. My father woke me up in our driveway.

"Never a word of this to anyone," he told me. "Not your mother, not your friends – nobody. You're cured of this thing now, and I never want to hear about it again."

As he spoke, he reached down and fingered his belt, threatening me.

I nodded and said I understood.

But I didn't, and never would – not really.

~

After that day, I ran into the arms of my only two only escapes: sailing, and books. Sailing, because it was the only time I was ever alone; and books, because reading was the only time I never had to listen to the thoughts in my head.

My mother was a bookworm, always lost in her romances. I always assumed she read her books to wander: to explore new worlds, to meet new friends, to experience new places.

But soon I learned *I* read for different reasons.

In that "doctor's session," I had been confronted with a new fact: the person I was, the human I was at my essence, was shameful and unnatural and wrong. I was taught to hate my own feelings. So I opened a book and never dealt with actual humans, or feelings, again.

Yes, some people read books to wander.

But me? I read them to disappear.

And that's what I did: disappear into my own mind.

Until I met Tommy, the boy who broke me open…

Once we set sail and hit the open ocean, headed due north-northeast, I avoided Tommy for two days. I just couldn't face him. He was so beautiful, it thrilled and terrified me.

Of course I'd steal glances here and there, though. Or...whenever I could, to be more honest. He really did have eyes like moonlight: most grey eyes had a blue-ish hue to them, but Tommy's were so grey and bright, they were almost silver, like the surface of the moon. So "moonlight eyes" – that's the name I gave him in my head.

He was tall and lanky, and was probably a year north or south of twenty, like me. Whenever he took off his shirt, which was quite often, his chest looked strong and sinewy in a way that made me shiver. He was also the first biracial person I had ever really been around. I didn't care, obviously, but something in the back of my mind made me wonder if he felt safe and comfortable around me. I hoped he did.

"Hey," he finally said one day when we were fixing some dry-rot at the bow.

Everything in me stopped moving.

"Oh," I said. "Hi."

He set down his rag. "So. If we're going to be stuck on this boat together until Maine, I reckon we should at least talk a little, yeah?" he asked me. "Think you could put those books down for one second and say hello?"

I set down my book, a Hemingway title I can't quite recall. "Sorry," I said. "And...talk? About what?"

"Hm. Tell me something interesting about yourself."

"I...can't think of anything."

"I can," he said. "You can tie a bowline knot like nobody's business."

"I can?" I asked, and he nodded. It shocked me that he had even noticed anything about me. I didn't figure I was even worth being noticed. But there he was, *noticing*...

"Your knots, they're very clean," he said. "You sail a lot, I reckon?"

"Since I was a boy," I said. "Our house was down by the St. Johns River. My granddaddy bought me a dinghy for my birthday one day, and from then on, I was gone every day."

"Alone?"

8

"I suppose."

"Why, exactly?" he asked.

"I suppose…I suppose being alone was the point. It was the only time I didn't have to be around other people and their…their ideas."

Tommy frowned. "Ideas?"

I shook my head and realized I was giving away too much. "Never mind. Hey, why do *you* sail?"

"Because…because the ocean doesn't care about what I look like," he said quietly. "The winds would never refuse to fill my sails because of the color of my skin. Out here, I can just…*be*."

I just breathed. I would never claim to understand his struggles associated with race. But the underlying essence; the idea of wanting to run out to the sea because it's the only place you could be yourself – I understood it down to my core.

"I don't care, either," I said quietly. "I hope you knew that."

"Of course I did. You're not like most people, space boy."

I smiled and then realized I was letting myself get close. I got up and stretched. "Hey, I'm gonna start on dinner."

Down in the galley, I stared down at the burner as it started heating. I reached down and touched it just to feel the burn.

~

The next day, I took a break from polishing the compass and headed to our only water source on deck, a hose attached to the freshwater tank. I walked up and saw Tommy already drinking from the hose, though, so I muttered "sorry" and started to turn around.

Something came over his face. He made direct eye contact and then beckoned me forward with his finger.

"I'll share," he said.

First, I froze. Then I crept closer, my pulse quickening as I approached.

I stopped only inches from him.

"Closer," he said.

I leaned in. He did, too. When my lips hit the water from the hose, only centimeters separated our mouths as we drank together. I could feel his breath on my lips; I could feel the warmth of his body. My heart was working overdrive, and my skin felt like it was screaming. It was the most erotic thing I'd ever done.

When we were both finished drinking, he set down the hose wordlessly and then turned off the spigot. As I watched him walk away, I realized I'd never wanted anything more in my entire life.

I think we both knew what was coming.

As I cooked some hot dogs and beans in the tiny galley a few hours later, still overcome with desire from the hose incident, I started thinking.

I'd been so afraid to talk to Tommy all this time because I thought it would make me feel…dirty. Shameful. Sinful.

But looking back on it…talking to him hadn't felt bad at all.

It had felt *good*.

And the hose thing? It'd felt like getting struck by lightning.

And I wanted to feel the thunder again.

A seed had been planted in me. And sunlight was breaking through the clouds.

When I finished cooking, I called up through a porthole offering him a hot dog. Tommy sauntered down the steps, looking too beautiful to be real.

Then the memory hit me:

Bzzzt.

I could feel the wires on my wrists; I could feel the electricity coursing through my body.

It was like I was back in that room again.

But I shook my head and pushed the memories away.

All I was doing was *looking* at Tommy.

There was no shame in *looking*…

Right?

We ate dinner in silence. He still just made me too nervous to speak – I was wonderstruck by him. After we finally made some small talk about the boat, he got a gleam in his eye and leaned in.

"Hey, space boy. I snuck some bourbon in my bag, you know."

I inhaled. "Well…"

"Yes?"

"Mr. Garrison said neither of us can drink on the job. We might get sloppy and stray off course or something…"

He sat back and crossed his arms. He was confident in a way that made me feel envious and sexual at the same time. "Try me. I've been sailing since I could walk, too. We'll be fine."

He offered the bottle. I swallowed hard and took it.

We got drunk, of course. Rip-roaringly. Somehow we ended up in the front cabin, in the two tiny beds right across from each other.

11

He looked over at me. "Why do you look at me, space boy?"

"Look at you?"

"I catch you looking at me while we're working. All the time. But you won't talk to me."

"I...I don't..."

"It's okay, though," he smiled.

"It is?"

For the first time on the trip, he looked almost nervous. He bit his bottom lip. "The thing is, I look at you, too."

My lungs stopped working. I could not breathe. "...You do?"

"The truth is...well, lately I can't look at anything else."

A beam of happiness shot through me.

But I glanced away and tried to puncture the overwhelming bubble of tension suddenly filling the cabin. "Well, I'm sorry, then."

"Why?"

"I know I'm not really much to look at."

I glanced back at him. He licked his bottom lip again. My stomach flipped: watching him was like seeing poetry in motion. "I beg to differ."

"You really do?"

He seemed to struggle with his response. "Sometimes...sometimes, when I look into your eyes, I think they could drown an ocean. You've got some depth to you, space boy."

He leaned over and kissed me.

Bzzzt.

In my head, I heard the noise.

Under my skin, I felt the shock.

I leaned back and asked him to please get away.

"Why?"

"Because this is wrong," I said.

"Did you like it?"

"Yes," I said.

"Then what's the problem? I thought you were...*different* like me. Was I wrong? *Are* you like me?"

"I...don't know what I am. But...doing that stuff is wrong."

"Says who?" Tommy asked.

"Says...everyone."

He looked out of the tiny porthole. "Who in the hell will ever know? This isn't North Carolina. It's a sailboat."

"Well…"

"Come on," he said. "I like you. What's wrong with that?"

I gasped. *I like you* – the words felt like heaven and poison in me at the same time. I had never heard them come from another person before, not even a woman.

But still, here it was, right in front of my face: my biggest fear. Being attracted to another man. And having him like me back, too.

But then again, my dad wasn't around with his belt…

That doctor wasn't around with his wires…

So…maybe they were wrong.

Maybe this wasn't so bad.

Maybe I *could* try it…

I leaned in and kissed him again.

And this time, no *bzzzt* ever came.

And soon, we came together…in more ways than one.

I didn't know what I was doing, but at the same time, I did. I'd dreamt about this moment so many times, it was like I was operating on some innate instinct.

And the thing was, it really *didn't* feel wrong or dirty or sinful – it felt beautiful. It felt like coming home after a long day and setting down your wallet on the table. It felt like a balmy morning after a long, cold winter.

It felt like everything…

And it was.

It really was.

"What are we doing?" I asked after we were done. The bed was wet with sweat, and we were joined at the chest, facing each other.

My heart was still thundering like a July storm. I had never felt so alive. It was like everything before this had been my prologue.

But I still wanted to know what this was. I was still confused.

"I don't know," Tommy said. "But I like it."

"What if someone finds out?"

He looked around. "Someone ten miles away, on the coast?"

"True." I swallowed. "I was wondering about something else. Have you ever done this…with another…"

"With another fella?"

I nodded.

"Well. I used to smooch a guy back in grammar school, in the woods behind the field. We'd meet up and mess around a little. It was nothing like *that*, though."

I want to find that boy and kill him with my hands – the thought came to me so suddenly and viciously, it stunned me. I had never felt so possessive about anyone or anything in my life.

I filed it away.

"Nobody can know," I said soon.

"*Obviously.*"

I sat back. "Okay. Kiss me again."

"Yeah?"

"Yeah."

And we came together again.

Ever since I could remember, I had believed I did not deserve to get away with happiness.

That night, Tommy made me happy…

And for the first time, I let myself feel it.

~

A new world opened up in me that night. A world of beauty and freedom and independence, a world with less fear.

14

My whole life, I had been trained to think that what I felt for other males was bad. But this was the first window into the fact that…well, it felt good.

For the first time in my life, it felt slightly more okay to be me.

The tension between my old world, and this new one, would be waged across the battlefield of my life for as long as I lived.

Tommy and I woke up together, in the same bed. The sun was bright through the porthole, and I could tell from the boat's bumpy movements that the winds had picked up and changed direction overnight, resulting in a higher swell.

"How do you feel?" he asked me.

"Like…like I had too much to drink."

Tommy gave me a look. "Come on, now. You know what I meant. You know, about…this," he said, motioning at us being together.

"I don't know yet. How do *you* feel?"

"Like I want to kiss you again."

"Wait," I said. "Please. Let me think."

"Think all you want," he said, getting up. "If I get my way, we're doing it again tonight."

Tommy started getting ready to set sail again, but I took a bucket of fresh water and headed to the stern, where I could be alone. Because I had a task to complete.

While we were kissing and carrying on the night before, I'd had an orgasm in my shorts before taking them off. And in the light of morning, I found it quite unsettling.

I ended up scrubbing the fabric so furiously, and for so long, I stained the wooden deck with blood from my own fingers. A long crimson rose, blooming across the weathered ochre planks…

~

I couldn't stay away from him for long, of course. After all, I couldn't really avoid him on a forty-foot sailboat even if I tried. We just kept bouncing off each other. Tommy was always singing, cracking jokes, laughing – and I came to love every minute of it. As they day wore on, I realized I *craved* it, actually, and found myself not wanting to leave his side. I cooked him dinner again that night, and when he got into bed with me afterward, I let him.

And then we came together again…

I know we looked like an odd pair from the outside. He was a dreamer; I was more pragmatic. I kept my thoughts close; he didn't so much wear his emotions on his sleeve as carry them around in his hands. But soon we formed a friendship that felt alive somehow – it crackled. Or *was* it a friendship?

I didn't know *what* it was, but we started talking about our childhoods and our families; our futures and our fears. He'd always say more than me, but I'd hang onto every word anyway – and I don't think he minded my quiet nature, either. We complemented each other. Once he mentioned that he'd always felt like he annoyed people, but around me, he felt like he was just fine.

And I knew exactly what he meant. I'd always felt like I was not enough for people – too small, too boring, too dull. But he filled up the air around him, and it drew me in like a fireplace on a cold day. He filled in all the cracks in me, I brought him back down to earth, and together we were a perfect match.

And around him, for the first time in my life, I felt like I could take up all the space my body required.

"Hey," he said one day when I was taking a break with a novel on the deck. "Since you got your nose buried in these stories all the time, ever thought about writing one?"

"*Writing* one?" I asked.

"Yeah, you're an eloquent guy. And you seem like a smart one, too. Ever thought about trying it out?"

"No," I said. It had never occurred to me that anyone would even care about what I had to say.

"Well you should," he smiled as he got back to steering. "I think there's a writer in you. Maybe it'll come out one day."

I knew I would never do it. But the thought that he even believed I could…well, it felt like being thrown a life raft.

~

The next eight days were the most perfect of my life. A brave, wild bliss. During the day we'd talk, play, flirt, kiss, as the boat sliced through the Atlantic. At night we'd do things I had only ever let myself imagine during my most private, illicit fantasies.

As we got more and more physical, the *bzzzt* sounds in my head gradually faded, but never really left. Sometimes all it would take to make me wince with pain was the touch of his hand. But slowly, on that boat, Tommy started healing me. Opening me. Freeing me.

Most of all, I just loved to notice him. Watch him. Obsess over him. And yes, obsessed was the word, even though it embarrassed me. But it really did become a deep, all-encompassing infatuation.

I'd never been so fascinated – or flummoxed – by anyone. Everything he did was interesting and confounding to me at the same time. I know he was open with his emotions, but I wanted to know more. I wanted to peel back every layer and understand every little thing there was to know about him.

I'd spend an hour watching him prepare a fish for dinner, and enjoy every second. He'd pass me on the deck and say one word to me – *Hey* – and I'd agonize over his delivery for hours. Was it a friendly *hey*? A romantic *hey*?

Tommy was a mystery to me, but one I savored trying to unwrap. Before long I came down with an overwhelming, almost feverish, obsession with him – and it only became more intense.

But there was something else. With every mile north we sailed, the dread grew in me. Time was slipping away faster and faster. And the little world we were creating on this sailboat – it wasn't real. The winding coastline, five or ten miles to our west – *that* was the real world. And we had to return to it. We could never take this little bubble and transfer it into that big, mean world out there.

The sailboat was an untransferable paradise, and I had to remember that.

The reminders were everywhere, after all. One day I was polishing the portholes in the cabin, listening to the news on the radio from the only station I could find, when the announcer read something that sickened me:

"*...in other news, today President Eisenhower has signed Executive Order 10450, which bans homosexuals from working for the federal government at all levels. This order gives homosexuals the status of 'security risk,' on the same level of other groups such as alcoholics and neurotics...*"

I jumped over to turn off the radio. I did not know if Tommy heard from the deck above, but I prayed he hadn't.

~

That night we attempted a sexual act we'd never tried before. But I heard the *bzzzt* in my mind and pulled away, bursting into tears.

"Hey," Tommy said. "What's the problem? What's wrong?"

"I need to know something," I said through my tears.

"Yes? Anything at all, just ask."

I swallowed and tried to calm myself. "When did you know for sure that you were…you were…*different*?"

He looked at the space between us, and motioned at it. "You mean…regarding this?"

I nodded.

"Well," Tommy said. "I always knew. I didn't look at girls in the same way I looked at boys. I just didn't. But there weren't many things I could do about it back then. I knew how it was for…fellas like that." His eyes drifted off. "Back in North Carolina, where I lived until I was fifteen, there was an older man who lived alone. Never married, no kids, nothing. People would already talk about him, but then another single man from another town started paying him visits. *Overnight* visits."

"Uh-oh…"

"Yes," he said. "My daddy started whispering cruel things about it under his breath. So did the other folks in town. Then, one day, the guy disappeared. Just, poof, he was gone. They closed up his house, and that was it. The official word was that he'd gone up to live with some kin in Maryland. But one day a few years later, my neighbors dared me to break into his house with them, just to look around. I thought it would be thrilling, so I joined in…"

I took a breath as dread filled me. "…And?"

Tommy took a hard gulp. "I was shocked. The kitchen was trashed, the chairs were turned over, and there was a pan of burned-out food on the stove. That man didn't go to live with his family. Someone snatched him out of his own kitchen, while he was cooking dinner."

I shivered.

"The worst thing, though?" Tommy continued. "There were *two* plates on that table. He was cooking for two. The other man – his 'friend' – had been there, too."

"*Oh*," I gasped.

"Yep."

"Those poor men…"

"I know. I threw up on the floor, and never went near that house again. So I just told myself I'd never be like him, and pushed it out of my mind. I dated girls here and there, and it was fine, I guess. I never even *thought* of touching another guy…until you, at least."

The truth hovered between us like a ghost: this thing we had going, it could kill us.

It could *kill* us.

That's when I broke down and told him the story about the wires.

When I finished, Tommy was stunned.

"James, do you understand what that is?" he asked me.

I shook my head.

"It is electro-shock therapy, James. It is torture. I read about how they're giving it to the suspected Commies, to make them confess."

"I don't know about that."

He bit his lip. "Man, oh, man. I could kill your daddy."

"Tommy," I urged. "Never say a word of this to anyone. He'd kill me, first. He's threatened as much."

Tommy looked away. "Well, that makes a few things make sense."

"Like what?"

"The way you seem…well, scared of me sometimes, when I touch you. You go back to that room, don't you? In there," he said, pointing at my head.

I nodded.

"I wish I could take that memory away from you," he said. "I know I can't. And I know I'll never forget seeing those two plates on that table, side by side, waiting for a dinner that would never come."

A long silence stretched between us.

"I figured you'd be in a mood tonight, anyway," Tommy finally said. "I heard the radio report today."

"Goddamn, I'd hoped you didn't."

"I did. And I was thinking. Why are we such a *problem* to the world? Why does it matter so much?"

I winced. The word *we* – I'd never heard myself be grouped in with homosexuals in that way, and it unsettled me deeply.

"I don't know," I said. "But it does. It does matter. We can't pretend it doesn't."

"There are places where it doesn't," Tommy said in a different tone. "Not as much, at least. My Nana went to Manhattan and said she saw a bar for homosexuals, and it wasn't even hidden that much."

"Oh, wake up," I said. "Manhattan is not Florida."

"Well would you ever...would you ever leave?"

"Tommy. With what money?"

He didn't answer.

"My life is in Florida," I said. "My family, too."

"Yeah, yeah."

I wrapped my arms around my knees. "I just wish loving people didn't have to be so hard."

"Love is easy," Tommy said sadly. "Love isn't the problem. It's the *world* that is hard on love."

Our last morning together dawned bright, clear, and chilly. I could hear the steady hum of the engine, which meant the wind had changed direction again, and that we could no longer rely on wind power.

That was the thing about sailing. And life, too. You never know where the winds were going to take you. You were always, always, always at the mercy of circumstances you could not control…

I wrapped myself in the blanket and went up to the deck to find Tommy. The rolling, low hills of Maine were just to the west, and it was the most beautiful thing I had ever seen. Still, I knew that sight meant we were approaching Portland, our destination, and that our time together was about to end.

"So," he said when I sat next to him at the bow, our feet hanging over the sea.

"So. I'm guessing the winds changed."

"Indeed," he said sadly. "They did."

We sat there for a moment. He rested his leg against mine. This time, no *bzzzt* sound ever came. It made me gasp and think about something.

In my mom's romances I used to steal, the characters would always fall in love instantly. A man and a woman would bump into each other at a fancy ball, lock eyes, fall into instant love, and speed toward their happily ever after from there.

In that moment, I kind of had the opposite revelation, though: I looked back over the sailing trip in reverse and realized I'd been in love with him since the moment I'd met him. It had just taken me this long for my brain to admit what my soul already knew. I had disappeared into him, like when you watch a boat sail away from you at sunrise until it disappears into the bright white light of the sun at the horizon.

Sunrise. Tommy was, and would remain, my perpetual sunrise.

"What are you thinking?" he asked me soon.

"That I'm glad you're the one who got put on this damned boat with me."

He laughed. "I am, too, space boy."

The hills inched ever closer, and soon I got annoyed. Why did this have to end? I wanted to reach out into the air and grab this moment; capture it; put it in a jar like a firefly. But I couldn't.

"Whatever happens, I still wanted to thank you," I said soon. "For this week."

"Thank me? For what?"

"For your friendship. For your time. For your…your *softness*."

"Softness?" he asked, not quite getting it.

"The thing is," I began, "I don't think my family ever really liked me. They loved me, I suppose, but they didn't *like* me. A lot of people love other people but don't really *like* them. They were never really kind to me. But on this trip, well…you've showed me…well, you've showed me more kindness than anyone ever has in my life. Even the way you touch me, you're so…soft. And nobody has ever been soft with me. Thank you. You're the first friend I've ever had, Tommy."

He squeezed my knee. "Oh, kid. You deserve it. I wish you could see you through my eyes."

I waited. "What do you see?" I asked soon, in a tiny voice.

He smiled. "Someone who deserves the softness. Someone who deserves still waters. Not the damn storm you were thrown into. That we were *both* thrown into."

I sniffled. "Well, thank you."

He paused. "…How do you see *me*?"

"You are all I see," I said simply. "I don't know what this is, but wherever I look, there you are."

"Same with me," he said, like he was relieved. "You said you didn't know what *this* was," he told me as he pointed between us. "But to me, well…*this* is everything. You feel it, too. No?"

"I…I like being around you so much, it scares me. Sometimes it feels like my heart is too big for my body." I shivered again. "But then again – sometimes, I'll be back in that room in my head, twisting around under those constraints…"

Tommy shook his head sadly. "I'm so sorry about what the world did to you. It shouldn't be like this."

"I know," I said sadly.

And then we took a westerly turn, and the buildings of Portland started coming into view. Every new warehouse and townhouse murdered me all over again.

We docked at the marina at ten in the morning.

Mr. Garrison had booked us on separate trains back to Jacksonville, and Tommy lived an hour across town from me. But we were also separated by so many *other* things, too – class, race, the laws of the United States – that he might as well have been a continent away.

I did not know if I would ever see him again.

We turned in the keys to the boat's cabin to the marina captain, then walked to the bustling road between the marina and downtown Portland.

I looked around at the people, the shops, the cars. Back in the real world, my time on the sailboat suddenly seemed so distant already…almost like a dream I was looking back on…I could see glimpses and moments and snapshots of it, tones of cerulean skies and sapphire seas and sepia-yellow sunsets, but no full picture…

"So," Tommy finally said, looking nervous for some reason. "I didn't know how to bring this up on the boat, but…I know you're looking to get out of your parents' place, and I've been looking for a potential roommate. My aunt has a little bungalow down in Vilano Beach that she's looking to let out. It's a dump, for sure, but I thought it could be…I don't know, a little project."

"Project?"

"You know, for you and me. As roommates. We could fix it up, maybe."

I didn't know what to say. For one, my region was totally racially segregated in those days.

"*Tommy*," I began. "Would that…would that area even be *safe* for you?"

Tommy tugged at his collar. "James, it's the only house for a mile down the beach, each way. I know what you mean, but…who's gonna see?"

"All it takes is one person to see, and start talking. We both know that. You should know that better than anyone, after what happened in North Carolina. Come on, be sensible."

"Where did being 'sensible' ever get anyone, though?" Tommy asked. "My daddy was sensible all his life, and now he's a miserable drip who just drinks beer in front of the radio all day. I think we could do it. I think we could be roommates."

I looked from side to side, just to make sure nobody had even *heard* him. I already knew he was a dreamer, an optimist – but *this*? It was damned near delusional.

In those days, two women could live together just fine – "spinsters," as they called them, shacked up all the time. They would be considered friends, housemates, companions.

But two *men*? Two single men under the same roof? I could not even conceive it. Not there. Not in northern Florida, which was essentially the Deep South, culturally speaking. Two known, openly homosexual people – if they even were to exist – were technically barred from even entering most establishments there.

"I will not hear of this anymore," I whispered. "You know what they would do to boys like us. I don't wanna die, Tommy."

"The cottage is so isolated," he retorted. "Come on, we could make a try for it…"

"We could do no such thing, and you know it."

He threw up his hands. "So what now, then?"

"I…I guess we just…get on with it."

He tilted his head, looking at me like I was the most ridiculous thing in the world. "*Get on with it*, huh? And act like the past week never happened? Act like we aren't the way we are?"

I closed my eyes for a second.

I wanted with everything in me to say yes to his request.

Oh, a tiny cottage with him on the beach, with nobody around, nobody to whisper…

It would be heaven.

It could also kill us.

And in a way, deep down I also still wanted to prove my father and that doctor wrong, on some level. What had happened on the sailboat, had happened on the sailboat. And that was that. But I wasn't homosexual. I just wasn't. I could love Tommy and still not be a homosexual, right? It could just be a one-time thing, right?

Right?

I looked at my watch. I knew he was already late for his train, and needed to leave. So in that moment, I tried to take a photograph of him with my mind. I wanted to etch him into my brain; remember him for the ages. So I took in his long legs, his elegant mouth, those moonlight eyes…

"Fine, then," Tommy finally said, turning away. "I guess that's it, then."

"I'm…I'm sorry. I wish I could change things. I can't."

His face changed; got a bit lighter. "Ehh, you're right. Don't be sorry. It is what it is. Maybe the future will bring you to me again. I'm happy to have met you. Goodbye, space boy."

I pressed my eyes closed for a moment again. Then I opened them. "Goodbye, moonlight eyes."

And then he turned and disappeared into the crowded street, just like that.

~

I walked to the train station on wobbly legs. I couldn't breathe, couldn't think, couldn't talk. I vomited loudly into some bushes as a passing woman stared at me in horror. I didn't care, though. Nothing mattered anymore, and I knew it.

I got on the train and stared out of the window until it rocked me to sleep.

Part II
Glimpses of Him

"And I could be enough
And we could be enough
That would be enough."

-Hamilton

1959

I tried to let him go for three years.

Three years.

And I couldn't.

That boy clung onto my soul like barnacles on the bottom of a sailboat.

And I didn't know what to do about it.

Sometimes I'd go to the exact spot on the dock in Mayport where we'd met. I'd look out at the ocean and see him in the waves. I'd close my eyes and hear him in the wind. I'd take a breath and smell him in the salty air…

I did get on with my life, in a way; don't think I sat around and cried. I took a job as a captain of one of the tourist boats that took twenty-or-so people out onto the ocean to go offshore fishing for the day. It was backbreaking work, but the pay was good enough.

Time passed, but he never left my mind. I tried dating around my town, and every girl just left me feeling cold and lonely. The truth was, as much as I tried to hide and deny it, deep in my body there was a shrine to Tommy Houston.

I thought of him always. He played on a loop in my mind. Did he miss me? Did that week mean as much to him as it had to me? How did he look back on that time? Was he ashamed? Was he moving on? What did his life look like? Who was he waking up beside? Was he seeing men, or women? To whom did he tell his secrets? Who was receiving all that love he had inside him?

Sometimes I'd swear I could *feel* him needing me out there, missing me. Other times I told myself I was crazy. But still, so much kept us apart. We were in the same city, under the same sky, but a whole universe of circumstances swirled between us, separating us like a brick wall…

Finally I broke down and found his family's phone number in a phone book I got downtown. Every time I thought of calling, though, I'd see my father opening my bedroom door…I'd hear him walking towards me…I'd feel his belt on my skin…

But most of all, in those darkest of moments, I would still feel the shame.

28

The pain.

The shock…

Bzzzt.

And that's what made me hang up the phone, every single time.

~

My father died of a lung tumor in the spring of 1959. I did not mourn him. But about a month later, I got the shock of a lifetime. My mother was going through his final batch of belongings when she found a stack of war bonds he'd bought in the '40s and forgotten about. By now they were now worth a small fortune, and since he'd left no will, we decided that half of it was going to me, and the other half to my mother.

Instantly, I knew exactly what I was going to do with that money:

I had found a way back to him.

A few weeks later, I called Tommy's number with trembling hands.

"Well hello, old friend," I said when he answered.

A short pause followed.

"Well I'll be Goddamned," Tommy said, in awe. "It's you. The space boy."

I smiled, but I was still nervous. "Yes, just thought I'd ring you up. Are you…are you angry I called?"

I waited. Every second was agony.

Finally he whispered something. "I…I think *angry* is the last word I'd ever use."

My soul soared. "Good," I said. "Just checking. So. How has life been treating you, anyway?"

"Uh. Fine, I'd say. Keeping busy. And you?"

But I couldn't contain the news anymore. "I bought the sailboat."

"*What?*"

"*Our* sailboat. Well, Mr. Garrison's. I came into some family money, and I was reading the classifieds a few weeks ago and came across an ad. I couldn't believe it. The old man kicked the bucket, and the family has been trying to sell it to cover estate taxes. It's been docked for two years and is a wreck, and it'll take a lot of work, but you just wait – I'm about to whip that old girl back into sailing shape, you just wait."

"By golly!" he said. "I'm so happy for you."

I lowered my voice. "The thing is, I was thinking, and maybe...well, how about that project?"

"Project?"

"Well, yeah. Instead of fixing up that cottage you mentioned. Maybe you'd like to go out on the ocean with me for a night or two? Maybe work on the boat together, out on the sea, like old times?"

I heard him inhale.

"What?" I asked.

"James, I got married."

My heart broke.

"*Married*?"

He was quiet for a long time. "Yes, uh....*well*. My daddy found a letter I wrote to you, and never sent. Long story short, he made some threats, and I found a nice little gal from church and got things going with her. Catherine's great, you'd like her."

My stomach dropped. I was devastated, but then again I always knew it was probably going to end up like this. We both did. And so I understood why he felt the need to make these choices.

But we could still be friends, right?

"Well, congrats, I suppose," I finally said, hating every word. "But...I'm still interested in the boat trip. Friends go out on boats together, you know."

"*Friends*," he said slyly. "Is that so?"

I got a little quieter. "Tommy. I miss you so much, my bones hurt."

"I do, too. It's like I can still feel you sometimes. I still feel you, James."

I took a breath. "So it's settled, then. Mayport docks, Saturday morning, ten-thirty or so. Why not?"

I could almost *feel* him smiling.

"I'm already there," he said.

I swallowed anxiously and hung up.

Tommy drove up to the marina ten minutes early in a coughing, sputtering old truck. As he got out, a happiness I'd never known bloomed in me. It was a joy so deep, it hurt.

Tommy walked down the dock, admiring the boat, then stopped and stared at the stern.

"Really?" he asked, pointing at the new name I'd painted on the stern, over the previous name. *MOONLIGHT EYES.* "You could've been a little more subtle, no?"

"What can I say?" I shrugged. "I thought it just had a ring to it."

I know I told him I wanted to be friends, but the passion I suddenly felt was supernatural.

As soon as we reached the privacy of my cabin, we were all over one another. I couldn't get enough of him, couldn't touch him in enough places, couldn't be close enough to him…

I'd wondered if our explosive physical chemistry from before had been a one-time thing; maybe a byproduct of being young and hormonal and suck on a boat together. But if anything, it had only grown deeper and more electric. That "thing" between us, whatever it was, had sank its claws into us, and trying to fight back was pointless.

The undiminished urgency of it was stunning. And in that tiny little room, I let out three years' worth of pent-up desire.

After our sex, I smoked my first-ever cigarette while slumped against the wall.

"That was…"

"I know," he said. "Man, oh, man…"

I blew some smoke into the air.

"Why didn't you ever call me before?" he asked.

"I couldn't. I…just couldn't. I'm sorry. Why didn't *you*?"

"Your name is unlisted."

"Oh. Yeah. That," I said.

"Was it on purpose?"

"Yes," I finally said. "The truth is, I thought it would fade. I wanted to stop loving you. Clearly, that was a futile endeavor…"

"Wait. You *love* me?" he gasped.

"What?"

"It's just…you've never said that before. Not like that."

31

"Well, yes," I smiled. "I didn't realize I hadn't. Yes, yes, I love you. Very much."

Tommy closed his eyes. He just breathed, smiling faintly. I had never seen anything so beautiful. "I loved you then, and I love you now. And I have waited so long for this."

"But...you're sure?" I asked after a pause. "I know the first trip was...*intense*. But that *thing*, the thing we felt, it never...it never faded for you?"

"*Faded?*" he laughed, looking askance at me again. (Good Lord, I had missed the sound of that laughter.) "Space boy, Technicolor doesn't fade. Come on."

He stood up and stretched his body, which was slightly less wiry with the added weight of his late twenties. (Still beautiful, though, obviously. Always beautiful.)

"Let's set sail, space boy," he said. "I can hear the ocean calling us already."

We motored out past the waves, unfurled our sails, and caught the wind.

And together, we were off.

~

That evening I made him hot dogs and beans, just like our first real night together.

"Tell me about your wife," I said during dinner. He was wearing a tight white shirt that made me tremble with desire.

"She's...she's good," he said. "She's...we're very good friends, but she gives me the space to be alone when I need it."

"Why did you do it?"

"I...*underestimated* how much my family would care about all this. My daddy came down to visit and found a letter I wrote, asking you one more time to move into that cottage with me...he made it very clear what he wanted me to do. And so I made a choice."

"I understand. Would I like her?"

"She's…like you," Tommy nodded. "She doesn't talk a lot. And she reads; a book a day sometimes. God, you and those damned books," he said, laughing towards the small bookcase I'd ready set up.

"Stop that," I said. "Reading was the only time I didn't have to think about missing you. But about Catherine, uh…have you ever told her about…"

"Of course not," he gulped.

"What was it like, getting married?"

"It felt like…it felt like several hours of trying not to think about you. What about you? Any gal pal?"

"Nobody special," I shrugged. "A few dates, here and there. Nothing to report. Nobody that moved me."

His face changed. "Come on, change of subject. We're here now. Enjoy it."

We made love again that night, after we set down the anchor. And the next morning, we set sail again, headed for Charleston Harbor.

On the way there, we didn't just work on the boat. We read books to each other, I'd listen to him sing church hymns from his past, I'd tell him things I'd never even dreamed of telling anyone else.

We set down anchor in Charleston again and made love for two days. Two straight days – that's all we did. And we were getting better at it; learning as we went along. I was desperate to please him, and he seemed just as eager to find new ways to please me. It was the happiest time of my life – well, since the first trip, at least. But it really did feel like we were back to normal. Time had changed, but we hadn't.

We were getting closer, too; establishing a rhythm between each other; getting to know every inch of each other, inside and out.

The only thing against us was time. And those two days in that harbor slipped by like an outgoing tide under a full moon.

Our last night there, Tommy looked out at a glittering downtown Charleston. I thought of all the people bustling about in that town, living their lives out in the open…

"Were you nervous, when you called me?" he asked.

"Yes. I thought I'd waited too long. I thought you'd moved on…that maybe you'd forgotten me."

"Ha," Tommy said. "Forgetting you would be like forgetting to breathe. Impossible."

I smiled so big, I thought my face might crack in two.

"Would you...would you ever go out there with me?" he asked. "You know, go to town? Get dinner, go to a bar? Nobody knows us here, James."

I thought for a long time. "I don't know," I said soon. "I've never been...you know, *around* in public with an adult man before, alone with one. People might stare."

"They'll definitely stare," he nodded. "But they're not going to *kill* us. Not out in public. Not like that."

"Give me time, Tommy. Let me get used to this."

"Time," he said darkly. "Sure. Time. As if I already didn't just wait three years for this single weekend..."

"I'm sorry," I said. "I really am. But I had the time of my life with you, and I'm so glad I got the sailboat back. Maybe it was meant to be."

"Stop talking and kiss me," he said suddenly.

And so I did...

All night.

~

The trip home was sober. We were both downcast when we pulled into the marina in Jacksonville. I had to go back to my stupid, boring life. And he had to go back to...whatever life he was living with Catherine, since he wouldn't really tell me much about it.

On the dock, we faced each other.

"So," I said.

"So. What are we going to do now?"

I looked back at the boat. "Um. Keep doing this, I hope? I'm gonna need a boatload of help. Literally."

He didn't look pleased. "And just...pretend we don't know each other, in-between?"

"What else are we supposed to do?" I asked. "I can't meet your wife. You know she would notice...the way I act around you. The way I look at you."

34

His eyes drifted away from me, and I could tell he was bitter about something.

"What's wrong?" I asked.

"It's just that…well, my aunt sold that cottage I mentioned before, since nobody in the family wanted to move in. It's gone."

I rolled my eyes, but the news hit me like a truck.

There it went – our only chance.

Our only possible refuge, outside of the sailboat.

But we still had *that* much.

"Oh, come on," I said soon. "Don't look backwards. Not now."

But he wasn't done yet. "I would wonder something sometimes. Are you sorry that you met me? Do you regret me?"

"*Tommy*," I said. "Stop. I'm sorry about a lot of things. I'm sorry they see us this way. I'm sorry so many doors are closed to us that are flung open to other people. I do wish things weren't the way they are…but you can be sorry about things and not regret doing them."

He smiled. Then he leaned closer. "Come on, seriously, though. Don't make me wait three years again. I need to see you more. I need this. This weekend made me realize how desolate things were without you."

I bit my lip.

"James," he said. "We both know I'm right. This *thing*, whatever it is…it took us over. We can't change that any more than we can change the way the wind blows in our damned sails. Listen to me, James," he said quietly. "You're the only person I wanna be alive with."

I tried to speak, but no words would come.

"Alright," I finally said. "It'll be no longer than two months from now. I promise."

He smirked. "See you in '*less than two months*,' then. I'll be waiting, space boy."

I ached, I physically *ached*, as he walked away.

And in that moment, I knew I was powerless to him, and would be for the rest of my life.

The sailing trips continued. Two, maybe three, four times a year. We'd head out for nowhere in particular, and during the day we'd work on the boat in-between making love and talking and cooking. Quite gradually, we fixed up that junky old sailboat into a masterpiece, and within a few years it was a breathtaking sight.

Tommy's wife had a son in 1961. It killed me to know I would never meet his son, but I was happy for him, and Tommy loved that boy with all of himself. I knew he would be the world's best father, and that's what he was.

Soon, my life split in two: my time alone, and my time with Tommy. I became two different people.

Out in the world, I was still a ghost. I was the person I'd been as a child. The bookworm; the quiet guy; the loner.

But with Tommy, on the sailboat?

I was all the way alive.

And truly, my life on the sailboat was the only thing that made my other my life bearable. I did my best to trudge through and manage it, but nothing in the world compared to those weekends.

But they were only ever weekends…

And every time we parked the sailboat and said goodbye for another few months, I saw the life I wanted drift further and further away.

After one six-month spell of non-communication, Tommy arrived in his truck and walked up to me, like always. But I noticed for the first time that he was beginning to age – his under-eyes were growing a touch saggy, and a few speckles of white hair shined at his temples.

He was still perfect to me, though. He was still my boy with the moonlight eyes.

But still, it reminded me that time was moving along. Faster and faster, it was starting to seem…

And soon I realized that if I didn't make a big move, time would leave *me* behind. I knew what people saw me as: a lonely man entering his thirties with nothing to show for it. Soon it would become too late for me to even try *for* a "normal" life, and I'd become even *more* of a target for society…

I knew what I had to do, and it killed me.

When the chance came, I did it anyway.

~

Lily approached me at the marina on a muggy Tuesday evening while I was working. She claimed her father docked his boat there, but she couldn't find it.

We found it *extremely* easily, though, considering it was the only yacht in the marina, and towered over everything else. She'd obviously known where it was, and just wanted to come onto me. But it was somewhat unusual in those days for a woman to do things like that, and I admired her for it.

We settled into things rather quickly. Around her, I felt calm. Looking back, she was a friend, nothing more than that, but I did love her on that level. I don't even really know if she loved *me*, though – she was single at thirty-one, and she said her father had called her a "feminist" (which was a deep insult in those days), and had threatened to distance her from the family if she didn't find a man soon.

Was Lily using me? Probably. Was I using her right back? Probably that, too. But somehow, it worked in a way I never really understood.

But for the first time, I had a friend outside of the sailboat. And it felt good, despite the rest. So when she started talking about marriage, I swallowed hard and forced myself to listen to her.

~

One day in 1966 I cleared my throat. We were sailing up to Savannah for the weekend, and something had been eating me up all day.

"Tommy. I have something to tell you."

"Yeah?" he asked, looking up from the rope he was uncoiling.

"I'm getting married, too."

Tommy paused.

"My family is done with me being alone, with me being a bachelor," I said by way of apology. "They're asking questions. I need to get moving on this, Tommy. We both know I do."

He fell back a little, as if he'd been knocked back by a gust of wind.

37

"I knew this would come," he finally said. "It still hurts like hell, though."

"I'm sorry, Tommy."

"Who is she?" he asked soon.

"A nice lady I met at the marina. She went after me first. She said she 'liked my eyes,' whatever that means. Lily is her name. She is kind, Tommy. And she is the one who proposed. I said yes."

He hesitated. "When's this all happening?"

"September 12, down at the Methodist church on Beach Boulevard."

I watched his face. For one of the first times ever, I couldn't read his mood.

"Does she know about...?"

I turned away. "Of course not. Catherine still doesn't either, right?"

"She...*hmm*," Tommy said carefully. "How do I put this? Catherine has...*accepted* the boat trips. She stopped asking questions a long time ago. I think she just...is content in not knowing what she doesn't know."

We just stood there for a long time, watching the sunlight glisten on the sea.

"We can keep doing the trips, right?" he asked soon.

"I...don't know," I said. "I need to think about it."

"What does that mean?"

"I'll be a married man, Tommy."

"And I'm *not* married?" he asked me. "And haven't been, all this time?"

I swallowed and thought hard for a moment.

"Tommy," I began. "This is the life I always planned on. The life my family always wanted for me. I love you, I do. But what if this...what if this *works*? What if I actually fall in love with her? What if I was never...what if this was all..."

"Oh, for shit's sake," he spat. "After all this time, you're going to pretend you never loved me? You're still going to believe in your father's fantasy bullshit? You are a homosexual, James. You love a man. You've never even been interested in women. You can play pretend out there all you want, but you can at *least* accept it in private."

I turned away. I wished I could agree with him, deep down where it mattered.

38

I also knew I still couldn't.

"I hope she makes you happy," he said soon.

He did not mention it again for the entire trip.

~

I got married on a windy day in September. It was harder than I'd envisioned. I cried the whole ceremony, but everyone assumed they were just tears of happiness.

It was also the first time I ever saw my mother look proud of me. She was beaming with it, actually, from the front row with my cousins. And it made me wonder: if she knew who I really was, would she be proud?

I knew the answer would be no. But I couldn't stop thinking about it.

Why was unconditional love given to some, but not all? Why would my mother only love me, and why did society only accept me, under the condition that I agreed to pretend to be someone I wasn't?

Why was acceptance offered to some, but not all?

And who had decided all these rules, anyway?

The pastor had asked us both to pick a Bible verse to read to one another during the ceremony. Lily chose something vague about love that I can't quite recall, but I'll never forget reading my quote from the stage:

"Mark 10:9: Therefore what God has joined together, let no one separate."

It just wasn't dedicated to Lily.

Towards the end of the ceremony, something curious caught my attention. In the back of the pews, I saw a pair of moonlight eyes, just watching.

It made peace settle into me. He was there. He'd come. For me. And I couldn't imagine how hard it must've been for him.

Tommy finally got up and crept out of the church just as the ceremony was wrapping up.

I wanted with everything in me to run after him.

I didn't, of course.

I never did ask him why he'd come...

But I was so, so grateful he'd been there to hear my promise to him.

And I'd meant every word of it, no matter how rough the seas ahead would become.

1967

I lasted nine months before breaking down and asking to spend another weekend with him. I couldn't stand it anymore. I needed him.

We set sail just before dawn.

"I was surprised you even took my call," I asked as the sun started rising.

"Ehh," Tommy said. "It's nothing I didn't force you deal with, first."

"Good point."

"Do you love her?" he asked me, finally mentioning the Lily-shaped elephant surrounding us.

"She is…a nice person," I responded tactfully.

"Have you missed me?" he asked.

"*Missed* isn't the word. There isn't one."

"Are you happy?"

I swallowed. "I don't know how much happiness matters. But I'm happy right now."

Tommy inhaled, and I could tell he was nervous at what he was about to say. "Listen. I've been thinking, and I don't feel the same shame I did as a younger man anymore," he began.

"What?"

"You know, about the whole homosexual thing. What happened to those two fellas in North Carolina really scarred me, sure, but it's a different time. I've really been contemplating it. And reading. And seeing the gay activists on the news." He looked down at his hand, which was atop mine. "What's so wrong with this? With *us*?"

"Don't ask *me*," I said, then I pointed out at the shore. "Ask them. They're the ones who care so much."

"So what?" Tommy asked. "Why do we let the world push us around? Who said we were required to care? I'm not alien to the feeling of being different, James. Do you know what it was like to grow up with my skin color?"

"No, and I can't pretend to."

"Well, I'm already used to being seen as different for something I can't control, and I don't know if I care as much anymore."

"What other options do we have, then?"

He tilted his head. "James, you are not a child anymore, strapped to that chair. You are an adult, who can make your own choices."

All the sadness in the world filled me then. I thought of my mother, and how she had hugged me for the first time in my life at the wedding reception.

Only after she knew for sure that I would turn out as she'd hoped.

"*Am* I, though?" I asked, bathed in shame, hanging my head. "*Can* I make my own decisions? Because my whole life has felt like taking orders from some Goddamned rulebook in the sky. Do this, do that, feel this, don't feel that, be with this person, don't be with that person…"

I felt Tommy's hand on my chin. He lifted my face a few inches. "Unbow your head, James."

Tommy forced me to make eye contact with him.

"You're still not over all this, are you?" he asked. "You still go back to that room sometimes, still feel those shocks. Don't you?"

I nodded faintly. "Forgetting is hard," I said. "Even considering how much I love you. It's just so hard…"

"Listen to me, then," he said in a serious tone. "No matter what happens, I love you, and you love me, and that's enough. Isn't it? How is that not enough to trust? I trust love. Do *you*?"

I wiped a tear away. "I wish I could be brave like you. But I can't. I'm weaker, Tommy."

Tommy turned his head and finally gave up on trying to save me.

You can throw a distressed swimmer a life raft, but if they refused to take it, they were still going to drown anyway.

And I was drowning.

"Your daddy ruined you," Tommy said acidly. "I'm glad he's dead, or I would've tracked him down and done it, myself. But I no matter how much I love you, I still can't make you love yourself, and it kills me."

I didn't know what to say.

It was the meanest thing anyone had ever said to me.

But more than that…

I knew it was probably true.

Part III
Growing With Him

"Seasons may change, but we won't change.
Isn't it sweet, how we know that already?"

-Elizabeth Grant

My first daughter was born in the summer of 1969. It was a love I'd never known before – well, outside of my love for Tommy, of course. Lily's father arranged for me to get a job at a bank he owned, a real job, and my life got busier and more stable.

That year Tommy and I could only find the time for one sailing trip. We made it count, though, and sailed all the way to Nassau, where we docked near the marina and made love for three days.

But it was never enough. Never enough…

Tommy had been right about one thing. Society as a whole *was* starting to change a bit, and see waves of protests and rallies and unrest. But down in Jacksonville, I was only watching those changes on television and reading about them in the newspapers. The culture there had barely changed since the '40s, if at all. The "hippie" culture that later came to define that era in photos and in the media – that culture was mostly clustered in a few major cities, none of them anywhere near me.

Of course I was grateful for the racial civil rights revolution of the '60s, but Jacksonville had even resisted *those* changes for years. My city had schools and highways and monuments dedicated to Confederate generals and Klan leaders, and we were thirty minutes down the highway from Georgia. My father had relations from Minnesota, and when my great-aunt Edith came down to visit once, she said it "felt like Alabama." Nobody disagreed.

Still, time plowed on. Tommy and I both started passing more and more life milestones, the big things that defined an adulthood. Kids, mortgages, promotions, marital issues, marital fixes. And soon I had to admit I was no longer the strong, youthful man from that first trip to Maine.

Things on my body started drooping and sagging. I started noticing aches and pains in my back and neck I'd never had before, and one morning I looked in the mirror and found my first grey hair. For some reason it made me think of Tommy.

The older you got, the faster time slipped by. In the mid-seventies, my wife had two more girls in a two-year period that nearly broke my neck with whiplash. Tommy himself had two sons, after which his wife announced she was done. But we had families now, real family units, and soon I started to feel like a real adult. But through it all, Tommy still remained my constant, my rock, my foundation, and our trips together sustained me.

He was just totally separate from that life; a moon revolving around my whole existence.

Not that I *never* saw him. In one year we did manage to sneak away for five different weekends. I always made sure the kids were cared for and Lily was okay, but soon it seemed like she *preferred* me being gone – she enjoyed her alone time, and I understood, and did not ask questions.

We were lying on a raft in the ocean one day, next to the sailboat, when I saw another grey hair in my reflection in Tommy's sunglasses.

"Tommy?" I asked, resting against him.

"Hm?"

"How much of our relationship is based on our sex?"

"*What*?" he asked.

"I know I'm starting to not look like that boy I was when we met. Will you still want me when I look *nothing* like him?"

He playfully slapped my leg a little. "Space boy. Age will come for us all. I'm gonna get old, too. If you think the way you look has anything to do with how I feel for you, maybe you don't know me like I thought you did."

"Sorry. I guess I'm just being insecure…"

Tommy put his hand on my leg. "If I didn't want you anymore, would I do…*this*?" he asked, inching up my leg as my breath hitched. "Or…*this*?" he asked, resting his hand on my penis, which stirred to life.

"Okay, point taken. Thank you for loving me, Tommy."

"No need to thank me for something I didn't choose. It was inevitable, space boy. Yesterday, today, tomorrow. I'll still feel this way."

And that did it. We got so frisky, so quickly, the raft ended up tipping right over, sending us both tumbling into the Atlantic together.

The excitement of the bicentennial in 1976 ruled that whole year, and Lily's parents wanted her to take the girls up to their beach house on Lake Lanier for the big holiday – meaning I had a whole week with Tommy.

It was the longest period I'd ever spent with him. We'd take the little dinghy strapped to the deck and row it out into the open sea, spending the days swimming and fishing and diving into the Atlantic. He gave me a ring that week; handed it to me as we sat under the sun. I did not ask what it meant. I just put it on my right ring finger, and never took it off. Ever.

We had to head back home a day early because of an approaching storm, though. We docked in our marina and made love all night, eager to use up every possible moment.

I was paying the marina fees at the desk the next morning when the elderly male attendant suddenly gave me a cold, hateful look; a look I had gotten many times in my life, and would recognize anywhere.

A look that said this: *I know what you are.*

I gave him the money, and he snatched it away, like he didn't even want to touch me. I had to maintain a good relationship with him, though, as he could revoke my boat's spot at any point if he wanted. Part of me knew I had to figure out what exactly had offended him.

"Everything alright?" I asked, and his eyes narrowed.

"Got a noise complaint last night," he said quietly, suspiciously. "The folks in the slip next to you reported hours and hours of banging sounds, like two people were making whoopie all night."

My chest seized up. "Oh, I don't…I don't know about that…maybe my generator was acting up…"

"It's funny," he said even more suspiciously. "For years now, you two fellas will head out together, and return together. Never any women. Never any wives."

Fuck you, I wanted to tell him. *Fuck you, and focus on your own shitty little life.*

But I just took the receipt and walked away.

I could say no such things, and I knew it.

"What happened?" Tommy asked when I returned to the boat, reading my mood. "What's wrong?"

"Nothing," I said. "Nothing at all…well, nothing I can change, at least…"

46

~

The mid-to-late seventies brought the curse known as Anita Bryant and the rising wave of backlash against the tiny victories the gay activists were making out there. Anita was a fundamentalist lunatic, but she was steadily gathering fame as a fire-and-brimstone crusader against the evil homosexuals and their insidious agenda. (An agenda which she never even seemed to be able to describe or explain, by the way. Evidently the homosexuals just had some mysterious agenda, and that was it.)

Anyway. Society was edging forward in some small ways regarding queer issues, and the religious right was starting to mobilize and push back. Anita was ranting on my television one day about passing some stupid anti-gay bill in Miami when I realized I couldn't take it anymore, turned off the TV, and called Tommy, desperate to see him.

But from the moment we set sail that weekend, he was gruff and curt and annoyed.

We set down anchor on a secluded marsh in Georgia and cast out some fishing lines. But nothing was biting, and his annoyance only grew.

"I don't know if I can do this anymore," he finally said.

I looked over. He was crying.

"Tommy, what's wrong?" I asked him, wrapping him up. But he remained tense.

"*This* is what's wrong," he said, looking down at my arms. "You've never even touched me off of this fucking sailboat. You wouldn't even look me in the eye when we were preparing the boat for the trip."

I didn't want him to know the marina operator had figured us out, and I didn't know what to say.

"I'm sorry," I finally told him. "I was just in a rush…"

"Well, some affection would be nice every once in a while."

"Well, whoop-de-doo," I said, my temper rising. "Sounds wonderful. Why don't we just go all the way, then? Two men, doing the kissy-kissy down at the marina, in front of dozens of people. Sounds like it'd be a fun scene! We might even get joint funerals, if they take pity on us!"

Tommy scowled at me.

47

"Look. I know this is hard," he said soon. "But that's the problem. I need you, James. I need you every day. This isn't enough for me. I barely know my own wife anymore, and my sons barely want to spend time with me because I'm so...so distant. You have no idea how lonely I get. I wish...I wish I could've gotten through to you. I wish I knew how to be enough for you."

I blew out some air, but really I wanted to sob for him. "You *are* enough. I wish I knew how to fix this."

"But we can't. And that leaves us with...*this*," he said, slapping the deck. "This sailboat is the only place I've ever been with you, James. Only ever here. The other day I was filling out the paperwork for my new mortgage and I thought to myself, *Is this really what my life has become?* I wanted...well, way back when, I wanted to climb hills with you and walk through cities with you and maybe even, I don't know, *just go out to fucking dinner somewhere*, like any normal couple gets to do. But all we have is this *fucking* sailboat..."

I just let him sit there, and I felt his anger dissipate soon. I could do that; feel his emotions sometimes. I knew he could, too. He could sense a melancholy or anxious mood in me from across a dark room. It had always been that way.

In a way, we were one entity, living and breaking in the same skin. That still hadn't changed, after all this time.

"The times have changed a *little*," Tommy said soon, very quietly. "I just saw a homosexual activist in *Life* magazine at the dentist's office. There are a few places where we could...where we could be *us* together."

"I'm sorry, Tommy. I have a wife and three girls."

"Then get a divorce."

"And go off and became a gay dad," I asked angrily, "and ruin their lives and reputations, and cast shame upon our whole house?"

"I never thought about that..."

"Oh, lemme tell you, they would be laughing stocks," I tell him. "Pariahs. Tommy, this is bigger than just us. A few months ago there were some rumors about a fella in the neighborhood, and his wife got iced out of Lily's bridge club, just for *rumors*."

He stared at me. "I get all that. But...what about *you*, James? What about *your* happiness?"

Suddenly I sprung up from my deckchair so quickly, he jumped a little. But few feelings were as violent as being in love with someone you couldn't have, and I could not contain it anymore.

"Stop this. Stop this, Tommy!" I cried. "Stop all this wishy-washy, day-dream-y bullshit!" I pointed at dry land. "They've got it out for us. *They've got it out for us*, Tommy, and the longer you ignore it, the more delusional you'll become! People are dying out there. Dying! And yet you want to run off to California or Massachusetts and be homeless lovebirds together? Sit under an overpass, with only our love to sustain us?"

"It would've sustained *me*," he said quietly as the winds echoed through the empty marsh. "It would've been enough for me."

All the regret in the world sank into my stomach.

But I was still angry.

"Goddamn it, Tommy. Listen to yourself. You say I'm afraid, and I am. But I'm also the only realistic person on this fucking sailboat. If the only way we can be together is by running away from our entire lives, that should tell you everything you need to know about the world we live in. So stop with the nonsense. Just...*stop*!"

He smirked at nothing. "Fine, then. I'll stop. But I know you're not content with your life. We both know that. You're lonely, and you know it."

Suddenly I broke down. I slumped and said the words I'd been feeling underneath the surface of my soul for years: "Why don't you go, then?"

"...What?"

"Why don't you go run off, get out of here, make your escape? Why do you let me keep you here, stuck in this life?"

He came over and sat in front of me. "James. Because I'd want you there. Right with me. That's the only life I want to live."

I looked away. "I hate myself for hating myself. Sometimes I wish you could let me go."

"Is *that* what you think? James, meeting you was the best thing that ever happened to me. I can't believe you'd think anything else."

I wiped my eyes.

"Okay," I said. Then I took his hand and decided to tell him something he'd told me years before: "I'm sorry I am the way I am. But whatever happens, I'm yours and you're mine, and I promise that's enough for me. It is. What we have on this sailboat…nobody could ever take that away from us. Nobody."

He closed his eyes. "Kiss me, James. I need you."

I kissed him, and we ended up making love right on that deck, in front of the entire empty marsh, in the middle of nowhere.

It was the most passionate night of my life.

I wish I would've known what was coming next.

1979

As I got older and more jaded, one thing that still never ceased to amaze me about humans was how damned surprising they could be.

My mother Elizabeth was a chilly woman, to say the least. My father could go into raging tempers, and over the years I watched her sort of shrink into herself. She also became almost hysterically religious, which I guessed was her way of looking for order in a chaotic life she could not control.

Soon, *Lucky Charms* cereal was deemed demonic, as luck came from Lucifer; the romance novels were all tossed into the garbage and called "the fruit of the Devil;" and when her best friend divorced her husband, Mother decried the divorce as sinful and never spoke to her own best friend again.

By the late seventies Mother's health was giving out, and as her only child, it was obviously my responsibility to take her in. Since she could no longer climb stairs, we banished one of our daughters to the above-garage apartment and gave Mother the biggest bedroom on the first floor.

I was alone with her one night, watching the evening news feature Anita Bryant on yet another of her tirades. I got still and quiet, as I always did when these issues were discussed around me, and just hoped it would be over soon.

"Can you *imagine* it?" Mother asked soon, shaking her head. "These homosexuals, just running around, *boasting* about what they are? I pray that the Lord will be on His way soon, because I know these must be the End Times."

Anger sparked in me. I could never address this subject with her head-on, obviously, but why couldn't I speak up a *little*? Why did I always have to be so...so silent?

"Mother," I asked carefully. "What about homosexuals wanting equality makes you think of the End Times?"

"*What*?" Mother breathed, horrified. "How dare you question me. Your daddy hated that. And why would you even *ask* such a question?"

But she knew why. She knew exactly why.

"Mother," I almost whispered. "I know Daddy told you about why I got those welts. I heard him telling you, from across the hall, all those years ago. I heard it."

She gasped.

"Don't deny it. You knew. You always knew."

Mother looked from side to side, as if trying to balance herself while the world shifted under her feet. "B-but…but your daddy said that incident was just two boys messing around, and said he'd found a way to fix it. Pastor Bennett found that doctor for you, he told your daddy he cured you…"

"*Cured* me?" I asked as the terror grew in her eyes. "Really? You think such a thing can be 'cured,' like it's a broken leg?"

She stared at me. "By God, James, what are you even *saying*? All of that is over. It was in the past. You're married. Why speak of it now?"

My anger intensified. If they had never taken me to that fucking "doctor," maybe I could've had a chance. Maybe I could've lived a totally different life…

Maybe I could've been *happy*.

Finally I snapped, and leaned forward.

When I spoke, I stared directly at her in a way I never had before, my voice icy. "I have a few questions for you, Mother. Did you ever think about why I would steal your soapy romance novels and read them in the bathroom as a boy? Why I never dated girls, growing up? Why I had so few male friends? Why I waited so long to get married? Why my marriage with Lily is so…*modern*, and why she lives so independently from me? Did you ever stop to wonder about any of that?"

Mother had been knitting at the time. When I finished my speech, she grasped one of her needles with her little hands so hard, it snapped in half.

We did not speak of it again.

~

Mother's health started to descend quickly after that. Her last few months brought a surprising new softness to her. She was fading, and she knew it. And she started changing. She started talking about legacies and memories and things we all leave behind.

Previously a lifelong avoider of pets, she started letting our cat take naps on her lap. She also adopted a new tenderness with my daughters, calling them things like "honey" and "precious" and "sweetie."

One day she shocked me anew when a Black postal service worker appeared at the door bearing a package. Her whole life, Mother had refused to deal with people of other races, and would send me to interact with whoever it was instead. But suddenly, she wheeled right up to the door, grabbed the box with a smile, and said "thank you, sir."

About a month before her death, we were watching the evening news together again when a segment came that made me stop breathing. According to a reporter, Anita Bryant had just caused quite a stir in the religious community by filing for divorce (which was still considered controversial in the South, even in 1980).

"According to her more conservative supporters," the announcer said, *"Bryant's sudden divorce announcement comes off as hypocritical, as her anti-gay teachings centered around the Biblical immorality of the homosexual lifestyle…several of the churches that hosted her previous speaking tours have already distanced themselves from the activist…"*

All the oxygen left the room. I was terrified of my mother's reaction, and braced myself for a litany of abuse and disrespect as I sat in the chair across from her.

Instead, she picked up her knitting needles and got back to work on her shawl.

"Well, serves that bitch right," Mother nodded, and I gasped again. "I'm glad she got what was coming to her. Good riddance."

I felt my jaw drop.

In all my life, I had never heard my mother utter a single curse word. Ever. And coming from someone who had once deemed Elvis Presley as "one of Satan's dark demonic spirits sent up from Hell to tempt our youth," it was more than a little shocking.

Mother looked at me then. Her face was now grey and pallid and drooping, but in her eyes I could suddenly see the Mother I used to know – the woman she was before my father swept her away.

"That wicked woman can't play God," Mother began. "She doesn't know what's going to happen to any particular group of people once they meet their maker any more than you or I do. She should've kept her nose out of their business, and minded her own." Mother took a breath and held the eye contact. "Now, listen here. I'll admit there's a lot about your life that I never understood. A lot you never let me in on. But I'm your mother,

James, and I love you. No matter what that *bitch* on the television has to say about it."

Yes, I was touched.

But I was also so tickled, I had to leave the room and giggle like a boy in the bathroom for a few minutes so she wouldn't hear me.

I simply could not *wait* to tell Tommy the story.

"I'm leaving my wife. I want to try this thing, space boy."

I gasped into the phone at Tommy's words. I looked around and then slid carefully into the pantry, stretching the phone cord as long as it would take me, until I was alone.

"Tommy. *What?*"

"I'm miserable. I miss you. I need you. Every day. I was thinking, and I don't want this life anymore. Let's run off to Manhattan, like we've talked about."

I tried to reason with him. He was always a dreamer, but sometimes he could get into these moods where he'd fill himself with wild ideas and become convinced of fantasies that could never become reality. It was like he'd gotten older, but had never grown up. I knew I had to talk him back from the edge.

"Tommy, first of all, calm down. Think about this. You have a life. A family. A job."

"This isn't living," he said, shame dripping from his voice. "I'm so alone. Every day, I feel so alone…"

"Well, what is this big idea you have?"

Tommy didn't speak for a while. When he did, he sounded embarrassed. "I've been drinking a lot."

"Alone?" I asked, concerned.

"No. With some friends."

"Friends? Who are these new *friends* of yours?"

His response was quiet. "There's a bar not far from my neighborhood, a bar that's secretly for…for guys like us."

I clutched the phone tighter. I don't know which was worse: the sadness I felt for him, or the jealousy that he was seeing other men.

The idea alone made me despondent.

"Oh, Tommy…" I said.

"Yeah. So I've been going there. Sue me. I've even been chatting with a few guys."

Resentment pulsed in my veins. "Oh, I'm *sure* you have. You've always been so charming. More charming than me, Lord knows. I'm sure you're quite popular."

"What does that mean?"

"Nothing," I said curtly.

"Oh, it meant something. But they're just friends, and I don't care. You can sit in your dumb little life all you want. I'm allowed to have some fun. I'm allowed to bust out every now and then, even if you won't."

I was hurt. Deep down I'd feared for years that he would grow impatient with me, get sick of waiting, and do something like this.

But I was also scared. What he was doing...it was reckless in a place like Jacksonville.

"Tommy," I said. "Wait a second. This isn't just about me. Think about this. Things are getting crazy out there. Did you hear about the fella from Middleburg?"

Tommy sucked in some air.

Recently there was an article about a man from Middleburg, a little town about an hour outside the city. He was found in the woods, dead for days. The article mentioned that he was a "recluse" and a "confirmed bachelor," and anyone could read between the lines and understand what the reporter meant:

That fag had it coming for him.

The police did not even bother with an investigation.

"What about it?" Tommy asked. "I can fend for myself."

"No," I said. "No, Tommy. Promise me a few things. Don't leave your wife yet. Don't make any rash decisions. Think about things first. And stay away from that damned bar. At least until the talk about the Middleburg fella dies down."

"Okay. Fine."

"No. Say it."

His voice got softer. "I promise, space boy."

"Good, moonlight eyes."

I paused and smiled into the line.

"I miss you," I said.

"I miss you so much, it aches. Still. After all this time."

I cleared my throat. "Well. I have some news, too. I was going to call you soon, but...the thing is, Lily wants a bigger house for the kids. She's making me sell the sailboat."

Tommy gasped.

"One last trip," I told him. "I negotiated enough time for one last trip before we sell it. Please?"

"Oh, James. You already know. Say the word, and I'm there."

~

We set down anchor in the harbor at St. Augustine, a beautiful Spanish town right down the coast from Jacksonville. I lit some candles and brought out some wine, and we watched the lights of the little village together.

I looked over at Tommy, and for the first time I could see the effects of the alcohol and the depression on his face.

For the first time, he looked...well, *old.*

But I didn't care. Even after all this time, being around him still felt almost like being assaulted by joy.

Still, a new melancholy hung in the air. Our little paradise was about to disappear. What would we do next?

I told Tommy the story about Mother. He found it endlessly funny, and nearly pissed himself laughing.

"Yep, she said it, just like that," I said soon. "Isn't it funny how people can change?"

His face got harder. "It's even funnier how some *don't.*"

I looked away.

"I'm going to be a grandfather," he said after another pause. "Can you believe it? Me, a grandfather? My oldest son knocked up his college sweetheart."

"Congratulations!"

"Yeah, yeah. At least the girl's daddy has some money. He'll be fine, but I wish he would've listened when I said to be careful about sex."

"Well, well," I said. "You know how people at that age are..."

"Tell me about it. I remember."

The moon started to rise. I thought about the fact that it was the last moonrise we would ever see on this boat. Then I shook my head.

Don't think about that right now...don't say goodbye yet...

"Look at us," Tommy said soon. "We're getting so...*old.* No offense."

"None taken. The other day I threw my back out, and couldn't even get out of bed until evening. It's all happening so quickly. Time…it slips away like rope in your hands when you toss out an anchor…"

He sipped his whiskey. "You know what I was thinking?"

"Hmm?"

"It could've been so much different for us."

"What could have?"

"Life," he said. "Our lives. Everything."

"Oh, not *this* again…"

He looked over at me. "We could've escaped all this. Back when we had the chance. Back when we were young. You know we could have."

"Tommy…"

"You know I'm right. I asked you all the time. I said we could've made a run for it. The whole world isn't fuckin' Jacksonville, James. We could've gotten in this boat and never came back. But you said no every time. And look at us now. It's too late."

I didn't know what to say. He was right. We were no longer the beautiful boys of our youth. We'd waited too long. What were we going to do? Start over in our mid-forties?

"The truth is," Tommy finally said. "The saddest truth is…if you would've made one call, if you would've asked me just once, I would've dropped everything and run to you. God, I'm such a fool…"

I didn't know what to say. There weren't words.

Tommy leaned against me, but his face was angry. "You know something else? I hate myself for saying this, but…sometimes I wish I knew how to stop loving you. This would all have been so much easier if I didn't love you so much."

His words hurt, but at the same time, I agreed completely on some strange, twisted level. "I know, Tommy. I know…"

Finally he smiled a little. "Hey. Remember the first time we kissed, on Mr. Garrison's boat?"

"I always will. That whole trip is a time capsule inside me, Tommy. I go back all the time."

"I feel you on that one, James. I feel you."

Tommy started getting quiet, and I let him fall asleep in my arms. I wanted to remember the moment, so I didn't let myself sleep.

The thing is, we do not remember most of our lives. A life, looked back on, is more of a smattering of diamonds shining in darkness than a straight, visible line.

Looking back, we do not really remember the days at work and the grocery store trips and the mowing of the lawn. Most of our lives fade into our memory like clouds drifting away while you stand on the beach on a windy day. What we remember are the alive moments. We remember the moments that remind us why we choose to keep going in this difficult world. Those are the moments that linger.

You remember your first kiss, all nervous and sweaty and triumphant. Your first heartbreak, and the way it shatters and flattens you like a glass bowl dropped onto a tile floor. Your first date; your first successful job interview; the first time someone ever told you they loved you; the last time you saw your childhood dog; the last time you ever held your grandmother's hand. We remember these moments because we need them. We need them because they sustain us, even the bad ones. They still tell us that we were really here, that we really lived, that we really happened.

In the years that followed, this was the memory that would remain with me: Tommy's warm body, collapsed against my stomach. The light waves lapping against the hull of the sailboat as a few seagulls cawed. And finally, the sun staining the eastern sky with hues of blue, then orange, then red, then exploding over the horizon in a brilliant kaleidoscope of a sunrise.

It was the closest I had ever felt, or would *ever* feel, to anyone in my life.

~

After sunrise, I slept in the cabin for an hour or two. I woke up and walked up the steps to find the skies cloudy, and the wind whipping at my face. The wind was *so* strong, actually, that a few things had been knocked about, and my boat's flag had been ripped from its little pole.

"Gotta head out early," Tommy shouted at me as he started pulling up the anchor. "They say a tropical storm's headed right up the coast."

We prepared the boat and then headed out via motor power, since the winds were not, nor had ever been, in our favor.

We parked the boat for the last time. Tommy sighed and looked around.

"So...no more boat."

"No more boat," I said. "I'm sorry. Lily still hasn't gotten her inheritance, and we needed the money."

"How will we see each other again?" he asked. "Checking into hotels could be dangerous for us here. Even I know that."

"I'll...I'll find a place. I'll find a way."

His lip curled. "I almost don't believe you. This trip felt like a goodbye, in a way."

I looked away. "I didn't say that."

"What do you want, then?"

"Tommy, we both know it won't be the same without the sailboat. Our lives are changing...I have a daughter in college, you're going to be a *grandfather*...this was bound to happen at some point. We were living in a dream on this boat."

He put a hand on my chest. "Alright, then. This isn't a time for anger. Just think on it. But James. If you won't have me in your life all the time, at least keep me in here. Remember me."

"As if I could forget."

"Ha. I feel you on that one, too," he kind of laughed. "I'll be seeing you, space boy."

"I'll be seeing you, moonlight eyes."

I watched him walk to his truck. Tommy stopped and looked back at me one last time, and we just stared at each other.

In my head, it was suddenly our last morning together, outside Portland, back on our first trip. Our legs were hanging off the bow as the sailboat charged ahead. The only thing out ahead of us was ocean.

He got in his truck and drove off.

1981

"Hello? Catherine Houston here."

It was a dreary morning in early January when I cleared my throat and prepared to speak to Tommy's wife for the first time ever.

Calling Tommy's house was something I'd never done before – he was the one who would always call my house, posing as a salesman on the chance my wife answered – but we'd had a sailing trip on a rented boat planned for New Year's, and he'd blown me off and was ignoring me. I guessed he was mad at me for being so busy lately, and also my jealousy from the phone call, so I just wanted to call and see if he'd answer.

But since his wife barely knew who I was, anyway, I decided to try to get answers from her, instead.

"Yes," I said, trying to sound as casual as I could. "I was calling about your husband. I'm a friend of his. See, we were supposed to take a sailing trip on a boat I was going to rent. I was wondering if you could-"

Catherine inhaled. "I'm very sorry you missed the service, but we're thinking about holding a family-only service out at the gravesite in a month or two for all my relations up in Chicago who couldn't make the original one."

I fell backwards against the wall.

"Hello? Is anyone there?"

"Yes, um...*service*?" I finally asked. "I'm sorry, I don't...I can't..."

"You didn't know?" Catherine asked. "I thought you were calling to offer flowers or something..."

"Know about what?"

Catherine cleared her throat, but it sounded weak. "I see. *Well*. Last month, my husband didn't come home from a trip out to a bar for a drink. His body was found in a field over in Arlington three days later. Suicide, *or so they say*. I'm sorry to be the one to break the news."

I slid to the floor.

"*Helloooo*? Are you okay?"

I tried as best as I could to talk through the tremors that were shaking my body, shaking my life, shaking my existence.

"Yes, I just...I'm so confused...*suicide*? But he seemed so...so happy...well, most of the time...but *suicide*?"

61

A long pause came.

"Can I be honest with you?" she asked soon. "I need someone to talk to, to be frank. Someone who isn't in my family, and won't spread this around."

"Yes, yes of course."

Catherine inhaled. "Tommy was a drinking man. Well, lately, at least. Something in him changed; my sister reckons it was one of those crises that men go through at his age. You know, that aimless feeling. And he became a gambler, too. Anyway. Nothing about his autopsy looked like suicide to me. He had bruises and...*anyway*. I made an issue of it, but the coroners were unbothered. I reckon they don't mess with anything that doesn't smell like outright homicide. But...my guess is that he owed a gambling debt to the wrong person, got into some mess, and they, well...'took care of him,' as they say in those Hollywood mafia movies."

My mind drifted off to the last time he'd called me. I could still hear his voice so clearly: *"There's a bar not far from my neighborhood, a bar that's secretly for...for guys like us..."*

My face hardened, and all the anger in the world filled my chest.

Tommy hadn't owed a debt to some gambling kingpin.

He'd owed a debt to a society that had denied him the right to live his own life, as he saw fit.

And society had finally come to collect on that debt.

"I'm...I'm so sorry," I told her soon, trying to keep it together. "I had no idea..."

Catherine paused. "Wait. Who are you, again? Sorry, all this funeral business has really scrambled my brain."

I wavered a little. "Oh, uh. Well. I'm an old friend of Tommy's. We sailed up the coast for a job a few decades ago, then struck up a friendship...we'd still go sailing every now and then..."

Her voice changed. "Wait. You were his...you were the...the man on that boat with him? Back in '56, before he met me?"

"Yes, ma'am," I said quietly. "Very old friend."

"And then...you became sailing partners? You own a boat now, yes?"

"Well, I used to. But yes, that's right, we were sailing partners, yes."

62

She gasped then. "My God…all his weekends away…the so-called suicide…the drinking…the bruises…my God…"

I had nothing to say. No words could meet that moment. It was bigger than words.

When she finally spoke, she was quieter. "He sure talked about you a lot, for a *sailing partner*."

"He…he did?"

A long pause followed. When Catherine finally spoke, her voice was cool, but vicious. "He kept the flag from that damned sailboat. Some stupid fucking flag, right under our bed. I never really understood why. I think I do now."

And then she hung up.

Tommy Houston came into my life. Then he left it. Nothing else outside of that had changed. Yet for me, nothing would ever be the same.

~

A few weeks after the phone call, a package came in the mail with no return address. I opened it up to find a tattered, falling-apart flag bearing the words *MOONLIGHT EYES.*

My sailboat's flag.

It *hadn't* blown off in the storm that morning, on our last trip before I sold the boat. Tommy had secretly taken it while I slept, as a way to remember us, knowing he might never see me again.

There was a note underneath the flag:

I was thinking, and I just decided you ought to have this.
I'm sorry for whatever happened between the two of you, but please do not ever contact me again.
– Catherine Houston.

I hugged the flag to my face and closed my eyes and breathed into the fabric. In my head I could hear it flapping in the wind above us as we sailed; I could smell the salty Atlantic air; I could see Tommy's victory smile and those moonlight eyes as we plowed ahead…

Most of all, I saw the life I could've had if I'd ever been strong enough to actually leave the sailboat underneath this flag and start over with him. The sailboat – it was all we ever had. And now he was gone. The sheer force of the regret hanging over my head felt like it was going to buckle my legs.

I never saw Catherine again, but I never did forget the breathtaking amount of grace it must've taken to send me that box. Like I said, people could be so surprising sometimes.

And trust me: grace was a thing I would need very badly in the coming years.

Part IV
After Him

"Love is so short, forgetting is so long."

-Neruda

2021

The morning after my phone call with Scott, I park at the graveyard and turn off my engine.

In the forty years since his death, I have never been able to visit Tommy's grave. Not once. It was too hard. I wanted to remember the bronzed beautiful boy from that first summer, not a plot of dirt in the ground.

But after forty years, I am here. And all because of Scott.

The thing that shocked me most about the call from Scott wasn't the news, of course. It was the lack of shame in his voice. The fearlessness of it; the casualness. And it made me realize why I'd never come to Tommy's grave: deep down, I was still ashamed of possibly being seen grieving at another man's grave.

I know it seems silly, but as a boy I did have to worry about those things. And even after eighty-five years, I was still afraid, still looking over my shoulder at every turn. Still ashamed. I never got over that.

That's why I broke down after the call: I was hearing, for the first time in my life, a person speak the same truth that haunted and tortured me forever, but do it freely and happily and easily. It shifted something in me and made me confront the one thing I could never grapple with, even in the decades after Tommy:

I'd felt from the first night with Tommy on the trip to Maine that what we had was pure and good and right. I was just too ashamed to admit what I already knew. I let the world lie to me and defeat me, and I swallowed that poison willingly. And I never forgave myself for it.

But Scott's brash, wild pride in himself somehow gave me the courage I needed to come here, and I'm finally doing it – regardless of who the hell sees me. I know I have to do this. Face this. And try to stop blaming myself for it.

As I get out of my car and fetch my walker from the back seat, an employee from the cemetery asks me if I need help. I say thanks, but wave her off.

This, I will need to do alone.

After twenty minutes of searching, I finally spot a stone reading *HOUSTON*. I stop in front of it, lean against my walker, and then gasp at the inscription.

THOMAS GIBSON HOUSTON.
FATHER, FRIEND, HUSBAND, SAILOR.

Sailor. I know he left a will behind, just in case anything happened to him, and that meant he'd instructed them to include the word *sailor*.

For me.

For us.

~

A few weeks after Tommy's widow called me, I went to the library and looked up his obituary. Of course there was no mention of me, but there wouldn't be, would there? Nobody would ever know about us. Not really.

I printed out the obituary anyway and bought a safe for it. I put in the flag, too. My little shrine to him. It stayed there for forty years.

~

In the first months and years after Tommy died, I did not know how to live in a world that did not contain him. I couldn't eat, couldn't sleep, couldn't function.

Sure, we'd only spend a few weekends a year together. But he was still my *person*, and his absence opened up a massive void in my life. And I did not know what to do with all that new echoing, ghostly space. I felt like a book, but someone had ripped out all my pages, leaving only the front and back covers to clang against each other. I was so empty.

I became obsessed with the past. In my mind I'd go back to the moments when he'd ask me to escape with him, and I'd go over and over and over all the ways in which I was wrong. And afraid. And cowardly.

The truth was, there was a chance – a very thin one, but still, a chance – that we could've worked out. Someway, somehow. Maybe we could've moved into that cottage in Vilano beach right after our first trip.

Maybe we could've chosen not to marry women. Maybe we could've left our wives before we got in too deep. Maybe we could've pooled our money and started over somewhere, made new lives, become new people.

Yes, it would've been hard. Yes, the odds were against us. Yes, it would've been dangerous almost anywhere. But we could've *tried*.

And we never did. Because of me. Because of the *bzzzt*. Because of the shame. Deep down, I never got over that shame.

My wife Lily finally left me in 1983. I didn't blame her. I would have, too – I was a shell of a man, drinking day and night, taking far too many nerve pills, moping around the house like a scepter. And there was no ill will towards Lily, either. We'd raised three girls together, and that was a legacy I would always share with her.

I had a few fleeting ideas about trying to meet another man. One night I even drove to a secret gay bar; obviously not the same one Tommy had frequented. But I was still overcome the second I drove up; I just couldn't face it.

And anyway, any ideas I had at "coming out" were totally dashed by the plague of the eighties. Unsettling reports of a mysterious illness in the nation's gay epicenters started popping up in the newspapers, and it only got worse. And soon, HIV/AIDS was an explosion.

I watched it all unfold in utter horror. Everything I'd ever suspected about the cruelty of the world was confirmed to me. No matter how loudly the activists shouted, the government refused to even acknowledge the disease – not until a movie star died of it, at least, and everyone was forced to finally admit there was even a problem. But millions were already dead, and real treatment for the sickness was still a decade away.

I watched half a generation of my own people die off on my television screen. It was almost ironic, if you thought about it. First I had to deal with the incredibly oppressive atmosphere of the midcentury Deep South, and then, when I was actually maybe considering the idea of "coming out," a plague struck down the very community I wanted to join.

And by the early nineties, it was too late for me. Or so I decided at the time. And I decided I never wanted to love anyone again.

All my love belonged to Tommy, anyway.

~

My obsession with Tommy, and the past, never waned, though. Every year on Tommy's birthday, I had a secret tradition. I would go to the marina at Mayport and stand under the palm trees on the water, and I would just feel him.

Because he was still there, and I could always feel him – he was everywhere in that marina. He was there in the gentle Florida wind; he was there in the undulating waves lapping against the bulkhead; he was there in the orange tree in the corner by the fence.

There was a saying Tommy would use all the time: *I feel you.* It was his way of saying *I get it, I get it. I hear you, I'm here, and I get it.* Sometimes I could still hear him saying it in his voice, even though many of my memories of him were already fading like old paper.

Anyway, years had passed. My depression and emotional paralysis weren't getting much better. My wife Lily had moved on and remarried; my daughters rarely ever called me. So on what would've been Tommy's fifty-fifth birthday, I walked out to the dock hoping to feel closer to him again.

But *this* time, I looked out at the water and heard a sudden voice inside my head say something to Tommy: *I can't feel you anymore.*

I gasped, because he felt gone. He just felt...*gone*, finally. In a way he never had before.

I just stood there, thinking. The love of my life was gone, and I could do nothing to change it – except get beyond it. But I wasn't. I was lying to myself by living in the past and telling myself my life was over. I was killing myself with drink and pills and depression. I had to get honest; I had to confront the reality in front of me.

I knew I had to deal with all of this.

And that day the marina I realized just how to do it:

I had to say goodbye to that damned sailboat.

~

I knew where the *Moonlight Eyes* was docked; Catherine had sold it to her boss and his family. I drove there one night with one mission: to say goodbye.

I walked out onto the dock at the marina in Orange Park and felt my shoulders fall when I spotted the boat. It looked so different. The new owners had painted it white and changed the windows. I cringed at the new name on the stern: *Sea, Sun & Fun*.

I just stared at it for a minute.

How stupid, I thought to myself. *How tacky. Don't they know this place is a cathedral devoted to Tommy Houston?*

A light rain was falling when I climbed onto the deck and started looking around. I admired the old dinghy we'd take out into the water when we were anchored in bays; I ran my hand over the ship's wheel, where we'd stood together countless times, trying to steer our way through winds that were never in our favor…

I kept exploring, smiling at little memories here and there. Towards the stern, I looked down and saw something in the moonlight: the faded crimson remains of my bloodstain. I'd left it after punishing myself the first morning after sleeping with Tommy. It was faint, sure, but still clearly visible on the deck.

I kneeled and ran my hands over the stain, which was glistening in the rain. As I did I remembered the shame I'd felt that morning; the sense of disgust at what we'd done the night before. I felt so sad for that boy. If only I could go back and hug him, cradle him, love him…

But I can't go back, I thought as the rain dripped down my face. One can *never* go back.

I stared at the stain and thought about things that remain. If one bloodstain could last decades, other things could remain, right? After all, I still had the memories…

I thought of my favorite book, a Hemingway story that was barely more than fifty pages long. But in those fifty pages he was somehow able to inject more heart and feeling and love than in all the epic novels I'd ever read. I knew Tommy wasn't here for long. But why was his tale any less important because it was a short story?

Really, if you thought about it, Tommy wasn't *totally* gone. What died didn't really stay dead. He was with me; within me. He'd painted a masterpiece in my memory, and I could visit it whenever I wanted.

And sure, I was just one person. But as long as I remained, so would he.

I knew then that I would always carry this grief. I had no choice. But maybe it was all about *how* I carried it. I could either keep it far away, like a foul-smelling bag of garbage, or keep it close and acknowledge it was there. But I had to get better at carrying this burden I did not ask for, and could not choose to shed.

And for the first time, I decided to accept our relationship for what it was, rather than mourn what it never could have become. And to remember what we did have, instead of obsess over what we could've had.

It was hard as hell, but I had to go on. There was nothing else to do.

I never saw the boat again. But that night did give me the strength to stop wanting to die. I would stay, to carry Tommy within me.

And for as long as I lived, he would, too.

I just never asked myself this: what about *after* I died?

"Well, hello there, Tommy," I tell him today, in 2021, back at his grave. "It's been a while."

Of course, the only thing I hear is the wind.

"You see, the funniest thing happened to me yesterday," I say soon. "My grandson Scottie called me up and, after about ten minutes of chit-chat, just said something like, 'by the way, I'm gay.' Can you believe it? Can you believe he was able to be so casual about it? Can you believe the world he lives in? Jesus Christ, it made me so sad…but happy, too. I'm happy for these kids. But God, what I wouldn't give to trade centuries with them…"

The tears come now. Suddenly I think of all the other stories like mine and Tommy's; secret love stories that will be lost to history, or have already been lost…

My God, the epochs must be shimmering with them.

"I have so many questions, Tommy," I say soon, through my tears. "I always have. Questions for you, questions for the world, questions for God. Life is so unfair. I don't understand why people are born in the times they're born in; why fate fucks some of us over and then blesses others. But…well, I *have* decided that regardless of *when* I loved you, I loved you with my whole body, and every second I spent with you lived in my bones forever."

I clear my throat.

"I want to tell you something else. I still regret every day that I did not accept your offers to run away, Tommy. I know it would've been hard, but…perhaps I could've saved you. Saved us. Times were *just* starting to change – well, in other areas of the world. But we had a *chance*. And I didn't budge. I was too afraid…too ashamed…the shame, it just…it took me over…and it all looks so pointless in the rearview…"

I start crying too hard to speak. I just stand there for a long time, listening to a nearby seagull.

"Let me stop feeling bad for myself," I say after a while. "Enough of that. You can't change what you can't change. But one more thing, Tommy. My grandson got me thinking, and…I just wanted to say these words to you, the words I could never say before: I'm gay. I really am. I'm…I'm gay. And that's okay. It is. It's okay."

I wait.

And then suddenly I feel it: eighty-five years of shame leaving my body.

My shoulders lift. My back straightens a bit. I breathe deeper than I have in years.

I thought I'd gotten over my shame when I said goodbye to the sailboat all those years ago, but I hadn't. Not really. Not until now. Not until I finally said those words. Letting go of Tommy didn't mean I'd let go of my own self-hatred. But...

I did it. I'm...out. I'm...I'm openly gay. Took a little longer than I'd hoped, but I did it!

And then I let out a whoop of laughter so loud, a nearby groundskeeper gives me a strange look. But for the first time, I do not feel an ounce of shame about it. Or about the person I am, in general.

I lean forward and run my hands down the gravestone. Then I whisper Tommy something had told me once, decades ago, during one of my countless bouts of overwhelming shame: "'*Hey, Tommy. I'm yours, you're mine, and that's enough for me.*' It always was, Tommy. I hope you felt that, regardless of the way I acted. Oh, and I hope you never thought I regretted any of this. If I could go back to that first day and meet you all over again, I would. I don't care how it ended up. Happy endings are for the movies, but I do believe in happy *moments*. And those happy moments you gave me, however rare, made the rest of my life worth living. You never knew this, but you saved my life, and that's a debt I'll never be able to repay. My time with you illuminated the rest of my lonely little life, and I'm grateful. Thank you, Tommy. Thank you, moonlight eyes."

I place a kiss on my hand, then touch my hand to the gravestone. Then I turn my walker towards the parking lot and trudge away.

Because there is still one more task to complete...

When I get home, I sit down at my kitchen table and start writing about a love story that started in 1956 and never ended.

I write for three, four, five hours. I write until it is pitch-dark outside. Some of what I write makes me sob, some makes me laugh, some makes me aroused, some makes me chest-splittingly angry.

When I finish, I hold up the stack of paper in awe. Catharsis isn't the word for what I feel. It's like I cut myself open and poured out all of my organs into these pages.

I always thought I would die with this secret locked within me.

Now, I know I won't.

And for the first time, I feel free.

I recall something Tommy told me on our first trip: "*I think there's a writer in you. Maybe it'll come out one day.*"

And he was right. It did. It came out.

I stuff my story into an envelope, and then I get my walker again and put the letter in the mailbox.

~

I will not bore you with the myriad of health problems that can befall a man of my age, but these days I am more or less being kept alive by an extremely potent and complicated cocktail of medications. Doctors have warned me that if I mess up my routine, or – God forbid, stop taking the crap altogether – I could be dead within twelve hours.

I pass my medicine cabinet without touching it, put my walker by my dresser, and slowly get into bed. For the first time in my life, I am going to do something on my own terms. I think I deserve that much.

Now that I have gotten past the one thing that truly always separated me from Tommy – my shame – I am not going to waste any more time on hopefully getting back to him.

I was never spiritual in the sense of believing in Jesus and the pearly gates and the little angels flitting about, but I do believe that love is a place you can visit. My whole life, I was able to sail back in my head and revisit my time with Tommy.

So who's to say I can't go back in death, even if it's an illusion? Like Tommy said once – how is love not enough to put your trust in?

After setting my glasses on my table, I close my eyes and cross my arms.

And finally, I rest.

I do not know if it is a dream or a vision or the process of my life ending and my brain shutting down, but the next thing I am aware of, I am on a sailboat. *Our* sailboat, the only place I was ever really alive. The wind is in my face, the sun is on my shoulders, the sails are fully unfurled, and the boat is plowing ahead, slicing fearlessly through the open Atlantic. It is sunrise again.

I feel a hand on my back. I turn to see Tommy, looking young and beautiful and restored.

My perpetual sunrise, risen again.

"Hello there, space boy," he says.

"Hello there, moonlight eyes."

"I feel you," he tells me.

"I feel you, too."

He smiles at me.

I smile back.

We both look forward.

And then we let the winds take us away together.

Part V
After Them

"These were the lovely bones that had grown around my absence: the connections – sometimes tenuous, sometimes made at great cost, but often magnificent – that happened after I was gone."

-Alice Sebold

August 2021
Scott James Garner

I stop at the grave, take a breath, and look down.

Two days after my Pappy died, I got a five-page letter in the mail. From Pappy.

Dated the day before he was found dead in his bed.

I started reading, and soon I couldn't believe my fucking eyes:

It was a love story, written out chronologically, titled *All We Ever Wanted.*

A love story between my grandfather...and a *man.*

~

"Shocked" isn't really the word I would use for my reaction. There wasn't one. My whole life, I never suspected...I never would've expected...

I mean, sure, I knew Pappy was single, and had been for decades. But I just thought he was a loner or a recluse or something.

I *did* know he had a secret – there was just something in his eyes that he kept from other people. I assumed it was alcoholism, and many times I'd ask him if I could get him out of the house or maybe take him to a local friend group for seniors. He'd turn me down every time, though, so soon I stopped trying.

But the *truth* about that secret in his eyes...well, it was difficult to comprehend, even for me.

The letter was also devastating. Pappy even included the obituary of his lover. He said he wanted me to know the story, to remember it, so their saga wouldn't be completely lost to history.

I didn't know how to react at first. I didn't know how to feel. So for a few days I just carried it around in my pocket, reading it every now and then.

Once the shock wore off, though, a new emotion emerged: anger. It made me fucking furious, to be honest.

But not at him.

I was angry at the *world.*

They should've been allowed to be together. Period, end of story. But they weren't, they were kept apart, they were forced to deny the only true passion they'd ever felt, and it ruined both of their lives.

Pappy said in his letter that after Tommy's death, he had these illusions that they could've run away and been together when they had the chance, but honestly I think that was a little delusional of him. He blamed himself when he should've blamed the world. Their lives would've been hard from the get-go, and their families would've excommunicated them. The odds were stacked against them from the start.

The whole thing was just so pointless and frustrating and futile…

It also made me think of how many *other* Tommy and James tales there were, romances that nobody will ever know about…

I was also a little angry at Pappy for never telling me he was gay. Well, in the beginning, at least. But as I read and re-read the letter, I understood more.

Their entire lives were contingent on agreeing to act like people they weren't, but even that didn't save them. I mean, Pappy's era was so horrible to queer people, they fucking *electrocuted* him as a kid, and the love of his life was *killed* for being gay. So in the end, I understand how those factors would've terrified someone into secrecy forever.

Pappy did not have the vocabulary and the emotional knowledge to understand this, even in his older years, but he was severely abused during that electroshock therapy, so much so that he entered a state of denial that lasted his entire life.

And I mean, no wonder he was that way – they literally tortured him in that session. They literally tried to train his brain and rewire it into thinking being gay was wrong. The effects were incredibly damaging, but he never really understood the extent of it. He never really realized it, or got a grasp on it. Not until it was too late, I guess…

But the last paragraph of the letter was a request. What Pappy wanted me to do was so devastating, though, I was hesitant for a few weeks. But I finally mustered up the courage, and here I am…

~

I take the tiny urn out of its box and stare down at it through my tears. (I asked my family for half of Pappy's ashes, and since they knew how close Pappy and I always were, they said yes. They just didn't know *why* I asked.)

But the time has come. No more crying. It's time to do what Pappy asked of me.

I lean down, then look around and make sure I'm alone. With my hands, I dig a shallow hole next to Tommy's gravestone, then put Pappy's urn in the hole, as he requested in his letter. Then I toss in his ring from Tommy, too, which Pappy left me in his will. (I never asked why he wore it, but it was on his right hand my whole life.) I also add the plain gold ring I got at Zales Jewelers for Tommy yesterday, since I know Pappy obviously never got to give him one during his lifetime.

Then I toss some dirt and leaves over the hole, hiding it all forever.

I stand back up.

But the floodgates open again…

Oh, the whole thing is just so *sad*. I cry for Pappy, I cry for this man he loved, I cry for a world that was so cruel, it made their love story end up like this…

What a fucking waste. What a gorgeous, shattering, spectacular waste.

It just shouldn't have been like this. But it was.

"I am so sorry for what happened to you two," I say soon, through my sobs. "If only I could go back and change people's minds…if only I could've done something…but I can't. It's done. You two didn't deserve this, God, you didn't deserve it…you deserved so much more…"

I wipe my nose and try to contain myself.

"So, Pappy," I say soon. "I want to reverse our roles for a second. I want to tell you the same thing you told me, on that day when I came out to you: you were perfectly made, and nothing was ever wrong with you. Nothing at all. I know that probably nobody ever told you that, so I'm saying it now. You are still *you* to me."

I sniffled.

"Oh, and I am still so proud to be your grandson. Always was. Always will be. I am proud of having your brown eyes, I am proud of having your name as my middle name, and I am proud of the person you were. I always will be, and nothing in that letter changed that. I'm sorry you never got to be *you*, but you can now. You can be *you* now, if you are anywhere at all."

Then I reach into my pocket for the *other* thing I brought with me: a tiny Pride flag I got at last year's parade. I stick it in the dirt in front of the gravestone and smile. Then I pat the little mound where I buried the urn and the ring.

"Good," I say through my snot and my tears. "No more hiding. Now you'll be together. Forever. In the way you couldn't be when you were alive. Again, I am so sorry. But you're both back where you should be, and I hope you two know it somewhere. I hope you both feel it. More than anything, I'm just glad you can relax now. That you can have peace. I'm sorry the world stole that from you while you were alive. Oh, I'm gonna miss you so much, Pappy…but anyway, oh, I just have to do one more thing. I now pronounce you two husband and husband. Congratulations, and have fun on the honeymoon, wherever you lovebirds are."

I take one last breath, then I turn back to where my boyfriend Jay is waiting, over on a bench to give me some privacy. And I smile so big, it stretches out my face.

I never thought about it like this before the letter, but lately I've been grateful for every fucking second I get to be with him. I never knew I was taking my freedom for granted, because this was the only world I'd ever known. I mean, kids started coming out of the closet when I was in *middle school*, and it was barely an issue. That's just what I knew.

But now that I know Pappy's story, I will never take this lightly again. I live in a world where I am allowed to be myself, and that is *such* a fucking luxury, and I didn't even know it.

In fact, Pappy's letter got me curious, and I started asking around. I told a Reddit forum for senior citizens that I was writing an article for my college newspaper, and asked them if they had any of these stories in their families that they could remember. I guess I struck a chord, because I was shocked by the number of responses I got, and by the fact that they contained accounts that ranged in tone from both devastating to downright heartwarming.

It seemed like almost every family out there had some version of Pappy.

I read a tale of a great-uncle with a lifelong male "roommate" who was still accepted at family Christmas every year like a family member, even though the context of their relationship was left unsaid.

I read about an aunt with a decades-long, live-in female "best friend" who was barred from entering the aunt's own funeral by her family when she died. So the "friend" stood outside, underneath the chapel's stained glass windows, and held own private, silent vigil instead.

I read of a grandfather who moved in with a male "special friend" after becoming a widower, and only after both of the men's deaths did their families discover they had gotten legally married.

I read of a cousin who would show up to family reunions for decades with a female "roommate" that the family steadfastly refused to acknowledge, even once. But she still came anyway.

And on and on it went…

In almost every story, the overall sentiment was the same. One man's response in particular seemed to sum it up: *These things just weren't talked about back then, it was more of an "unsaid knowledge" type of thing (if it was tolerated at all), but I wish I would've signaled to them that I was okay with it when I could have. But I wish they knew I accepted them. I hope they knew I loved them. I wish I would've said something…and it is so unfair that nobody will ever know the real story of what happened between them.*

The story about the grandfather in particular reminded me of Pappy and made me sob for an hour. If I could give every cent in my bank account to go back and tell him I accepted him while he was actually still alive, I would do it.

But the stories made me even more urgent to find some way to help. In fact, I've changed my major in school. I went from art history to English, so I can go to law school in two years and get my law degree. Everyone likes to act like the battle for queer civil rights is a thing of the past, but the more I pay attention and research and talk to people, the more I realize it's not over. I left my little bubble and opened my eyes, and what I see is shocking.

For instance, anti-queer bills are currently being passed all over the country, on the state level. And we need to do something. So if everything goes to plan, I am going to become an advocacy lawyer and do everything within my power to help fight back against these tides.

I won't let them take us back in time, back to when these stories had to die – I swear on Pappy's life.

Suddenly a line from his letter comes to me: "*It never occurred to me that I could be me until it was too late. I know you're already on the right track, Scottie, but if I leave you with one piece of advice, it's this: be the hell out of yourself, as if your life depends on it. Because it does. Take it from me.*"

"What's going on?" Jay asks me when I finally walk up. "Are you okay? How do you feel?"

"Awful, but I'm so glad I came. Let's go."

As I start to walk beside him to the car, I think of *another* line from Pappy's letter: "*Oh, what I wouldn't give to go back in time and hold Tommy's hand just one more time – but in public, instead of on that sailboat...*"

I reach out. "Hold my hand, please."

"Okay," he shrugs.

And then my boyfriend takes my hand and walks me to the car.

"So, are you gonna tell me what this whole thing was?" he asks me as he starts the engine. "You know, why we just brought an urn to a random cemetery, where nobody in your family seems to be buried, and why your face is so swollen from crying, you look like you got stung by a bee?"

For a moment I consider telling him.

Then I remember the secrecy oath that Pappy begged me to take, at the beginning of the letter. It was difficult to admit this to myself, but even at the end of his life, it still seemed like Pappy was embarrassed on some level. It broke my heart, but still, I understood.

He wanted me to know, sure, but he *only* wanted me to know. He wanted to pass on his story to a new generation, but he still wanted it to be a secret.

Then I think of one of the most heartbreaking lines of the letter: "*All we ever wanted was to be left alone. To be allowed to be ourselves. To be allowed to hold hands on a beach without anyone gawking or whispering or, God forbid, murdering us. That's all we ever wanted. And we never got it.*"

But they got it now. They're alone, finally. And I'll keep it that way.

"Oh, it was nothing," I finally say. "I was just doing a favor for a friend. Nothing important. Sorry I get emotional; I just hate cemeteries in general. Hey, wanna go to Zaxby's?"

"Sure," Jay shrugs as he pulls out of the parking lot.

I look back for one last glimpse of Tommy (and now Pappy's) grave, and something tells me for sure that I will never tell a single soul about their story.

Because truthfully, the world doesn't *deserve* their story.

The world already did enough damage to them.

Their story belongs on that sailboat, the place where it happened, the place where they loved each other.

And that's where it'll stay.

For good.

"*I promise, Pappy,*" I whisper as we round a corner and the tiny little Pride flag finally disappears from view. "*I promise.*"

The End
A note from the author:

In 2017 I received an email out of the blue from a reader who had just finished one of my books. The subject line read _TOP SECRET...PLS DO NOT SHARE._

It was from a male pastor in his eighties whom I will call John, and it turned out to be a gripping, powerful, and somewhat astonishing story of a secret gay love affair he'd had with another male pastor that had come to define his entire life. John was still a working pastor, still closeted, and still desperately in love with his secret partner, who had passed away ten years before.

John told me that my book had made him realize his story would die with him when he passed, and he was thinking of turning it into a book he could release anonymously. I urged him to do so, and we became pen pals.

Soon, though, I realized he was still wracked with guilt and shame over his gay affair due to the religious beliefs he still carried, and a book would probably be out of the question. No matter how many times I told him his story was important and valuable and worth sharing, I started to tell I would probably never get through to him.

He stopped emailing as much, and since I already felt like a pest, we gradually lost touch.

I never forgot him.

~

A few months ago John crossed my mind, and I wondered if there was a chance anything had ever come of the book idea. I pulled up his profile and saw nothing but "RIP" posts from family members. He'd died before he'd gotten brave enough to share his truth. I was devastated.

I was also very, very angry.

The truth is, history is filled with stories like John's. Stories that were buried under shame, stories that died in darkness. Stories that were murdered by society. Stories that will never be told.

For some reason I couldn't get John out of my head, and eventually his story inspired me to write a love affair that actually _would_ see sunlight.

All We Ever Wanted may be fictional, but how many times did the same story unravel in reality? Nobody will ever know, and that's the point.

Many people say we do not need any more sad, gay stories. I disagree down to my bones. We need gay stories, period, and to narrow down what stories we can and can't tell about our own experiences is wrong. Previous generations may have been excluded from "happily ever after," but to sweep away their stories and act like they never happened would be a senseless waste. If we do not acknowledge our collective trauma, how can we ever heal from it? When we speak, when we share, we can change things. Maybe even change the world.

John's story deserved to be told, even if it was sad. I wish he had shared it, but I understand why he felt like he could not.

Freedom is a privilege, but a responsibility, too. Our world is so different from the nightmare that John and Tommy and James had to live in, but we can still slide backwards. We are sliding backwards right now, in fact, in the form of the anti-trans bills spreading insidiously throughout state legislators today.

The queer trailblazers who came before us fought to clear away the clouds of their times to give us the sunlight we enjoy today. But let's make sure we keep those skies clear. And as we fight, let's make sure we remember and honor them. Because they were here. They lived. And loved, too.

Nobody ever knew that John loved another man with his whole soul. Not his widow, not his children, not his friends. And nobody *will* ever know, besides me.

I can't go back and urge him harder to write his story, although I wish I had. But this book is dedicated to him, and all the other folks who never got to live to see this world.

We will remember. But more than that, we will fight for sunlight.

This book is for you, John. I know you never truly got over the shame, nor did James. But I hope this helps.

-Seth King
2021

The End

~

Straight

Henry Morgan is a beer-drinking, arm-wrestling, 100% heterosexual American male – until he meets Ty Stanton, and watches all that fly out of the window forever.

Straight-ish (Straight, #2)

Henry and Ty are in love, and headed toward a serious, adult relationship. But Henry has never been with another man in his life before. *Now* what?

Liberty

After being forced to attend conversion therapy at their local church by their disapproving fathers, teenagers August Brees and Corey Ross lock eyes from across the room one day and then fall into a love that changes both of their lives forever.

Curious

Best friends Beau Lindemann and Nathan Sykes took their first steps together and went to their first prom in the same limo. In fact, there's nothing these 22-year-olds have ever kept from each other – except one long-simmering secret. They're sexually curious. After they both get dumped by their girlfriends just before a tropical vacation, Beau and Nathan have a boozy night together and make the shocking decision to throw caution to the winds, forget about girls for a few days, and make a pact to use each other's bodies for sex. That was their first mistake….

Honesty

Teenager Cole Furman knows two things. The first is that nearly everyone in his deeply conservative family disapproves of gay people. The second is that he is falling flourescently in love with a hazel-eyed guy from school named Nick Flores.

Sunlight

In the 1960s, Fred Ecklund meets a kaleidoscopic soul called Harry Faulkner, instantly changing both of their lives for good. The next three decades are a harrowing and heartwarming period of danger, passion, and soul-deep love under the oaks of the oppressive South.

Queer

A memoir by Seth King on growing up gay in the Deep South.

Brave

A memoir by Seth King on growing up with 17 siblings and eventually becoming a bestselling author.

All of the Colors

Seth King's first book of poetry

The Valentine Cabin

Liz and Corey are total opposites who suddenly find themselves stranded in a mountain cabin for the weekend. And before long, their hatred turns to passion…

Hopeless Romantic

After losing his engagement to the woman he thought would be the great love of his life, twenty-three-year-old aspiring writer Graham Herrera is in pieces. After four months, though, it becomes clear just how he can get his life back on track and reassemble his soul: write a book about his lost love and shed her bad blood forever.

There's just one problem: that would make him a "male romance author," and according to society, men know *nothing* about romance, right?

Wrong. And he's about to prove it.

The Summer Remains

Twenty-four-year-old Summer Johnson knows two things. The first is that due to a quickly worsening medical condition, she faces a risky surgery in three months' time that may or may not end in her death. The second is that she would like to fall in love before then. As spring sinks into her namesake season on the Florida coastline, Summer plays the odds and downloads a new dating app - and after one intriguing message from a beautiful surfer named Cooper Nichols, it becomes clear that the story of what may be her last few months under the sun is about to be completely revised. All she has to do now is write something worth reading.

Autumn Rising

Summer Jonson's best friend Autumn meets the man of her dreams just as she is trying to start a new life and get over the loss of her friend.

<u>Invincible Summer</u>

Cooper Nichols moves on after the loss of his soulmate.

About the Author:
Seth King is a 30-year-old author who lives in Florida.

Made in the USA
Columbia, SC
22 December 2022

73446879R00062